I0652257

Anonymous

The Vegetarian

a monthly magainze published to advocate wholesome living - Vol. 1

Anonymous

The Vegetarian
a monthly magainze published to advocate wholesome living - Vol. 1

ISBN/EAN: 9783337382803

Printed in Europe, USA, Canada, Australia, Japan

Cover: Foto ©Andreas Hilbeck / pixelio.de

More available books at **www.hansebooks.com**

THE

Vegetarian,

A Monthly Magazine published to advocate

Wholesome Living.

VOL. II.

NEW YORK:

THE VEGETARIAN PUBLISHING COMPANY,

40 JOHN STREET.

INDEX.

THE
Vegetarian·

Subscription:

Per Year, prepaid, to any part of the World, ... 25 cents.
10 Subscriptions, to different addresses . . . . . . $1.00.
Single copies, 2 cents; 50 cents per 100.

Published Monthly by
The Vegetarian Publishing Company, 40 John Street, New York City.

Entered at the New York Post Office as Second-class matter.

| Vol. II. | July 15, 1896. | No. 1. |

Diet and Happiness.

At the April meeting of the Vegetarian Society, Mr. J. W. Hutchinson, the best known member of that talented family of singers stated that "the best medicine was Joy." He is undoubtedly right. Sickness is unhappiness; health is joy; joy is love, and love is perfection. A person cannot be unhappy who loves his fellow creatures, and love, to be worthy of the name takes in all creation. Love of the individual is either selfishness or sensuality and is unworthy of the name. The scripture says "God is Love," but we do not require to turn to holy writ to learn this self evident law. Every instinct of our nature demonstrates this great truth. While we love we are happy and spread an aura of happiness around us. He must be a very bad man who could live among happy people and not be influenced by their joy. The reverse is true of hate, it spreads a miasmatic influence over all, blotting out every good influence and degrading all coming within its sphere to one common level.

As we cannot truly love our family without loving the rest of mankind, neither can we honestly love the human animal without loving the beautiful creatures which are animated with the same desires although expressed in different ways and emanating from different shaped bodies. The lark singing in the sky is spreading an area of joy as far as its voice can reach and probably contributes as much pure thought in the heart of man as many beings with higher organization who are apt to consider themselves the lords of creation.

Roman emperors are reported to have eaten dishes made of canary bird's tongues. Is it necessary to add any further testimony to demonstrate their iniquity; but people of the present day supposed to be civilized eat pigeon pie. In fact, the lusts of flesh eaters are like their other lusts, never satisfied, and ever looking for some new sensation to be secured at the expense of new victims.

Demonstrate as you may that man is possessed of an immortal soul, it is impossible to deny that the actual figure we see is animal, subject to the same general laws of life, death and happiness as his four-legged contemporaries. Why then should we copy all the vices of the worst forms of animal life and neglect their unfailing instinct used in the selection of food? With one solitary exception all animals useful to man are herbivorous, and are practically confined to one article of diet. Half the life of the majority of women is devoted to the selection and preparation of food, wasting the time which could be put to better purposes, and laying the foundation for ills innumerable, when they have finally succeeded in destroying the stomach which was intended to last through life in good repair. One class of food is sufficient, find out by experiment what is exactly suited to your stomach with its inherited weakness derived from flesh eating ancestors and then eat a sufficient quantity twice a day. Proper food selected from the fruits of the earth, be it grain, pulse, fruit or roots, will always be satisfying and is always enjoyed. You will never be hungry except when you set down to your meals and will always be happy because in protecting your own life you are not taking the lives of others; a clear conscience is the requisite of happiness.

Different religions and peoples hold many diverse ideas of heaven. I recollect hearing of the death bed of an old sailor who was being comforted by a kind christian explaining according to her ideas the beauties of a future life. She was interrupted by the dying man, saying, "But, Miss, it can't be better than sitting in a public with a fiddle going, tobacco in your pipe and plenty of beer." This was his idea of perfect bliss. Others look forward to a place rest, while my best conception would be a place where we do not require to eat, dress or sleep and can work twenty-four hours per day. I think this is the experience of all vegetarians; they are never tired, while flesh eaters living on an exciting and vitiated diet find it difficult to satisfy their hunger with a reasonable quantity of food. They are thus tempted to devour large quantities of unhealthy material which gradually wears out their digestive organs and leaves them after each meal in a depressed condition of nerves and muscles, unfitted for work and an easy prey for any form of dissipation which may be encountered. This is equally true of all flesh-eating animals, most prominent in the greatest eaters. The serpent will lie dormant for weeks or months after swallowing a large mass of flesh, while lions and their like will be almost quiescent for a day after eating. Herbivorous animals are never in this condition, they eat their food with pleasure instead of passion and are always lively and alert.

Life should be a perpetual joy from birth to death and this last great change should be hailed with pleasure; when having filled a hundred years or so with happiness and having accomplished all the good possible in this life, we hail with gladness the passage to another world where with renewed youth and an increased capacity for work we can joyfully start on new and greater tasks. That this will be the general condition of mankind I have no doubt when they return to the proper food of man and abandon the use of flesh.

The Drink-Crave—How to Cure.

By J. C. Jackson, M. D.

It is said there are not less than six hundred thousand habitual drunkards in the United States, and that of these sixty thousand at least die annually. In this reckoning is not included a much larger number of persons who are in the moderate use of intoxicating drinks, and from whose ranks the supply against the waste by death is annually made good. But how? From our children come our moderate drinkers; from our moderate drinkers come our drunkards. During the past fifty years efforts have been made which, for earnestness and enthusiasm, entitle those who have made them to the admiration of the wise and good the world over, to stay the transformation of sober, rational men and women into inebriated, irrational ones. A great many persons have been saved under the temperance reformation. Still, the increase of drunkards keeps pace, or nearly so, with the increase of population. It is fair, therefore, to look the whole field over from any new standpoint which close observation and experience may present, and see if some advance cannot be made in the direction of guarding and protecting the young against acquiring an appetite for intoxicating drinks.

It is certain that no person will drink without the desire to drink—the desire being always the prompting motive of indulgence. How comes it then that we create this desire for strong drinks in our children? I answer, we do this through our wretched dietetic arrangements. I have made extensive inquiries— and my opportunities have been unusually large— and I never found a man who was in the habit of becoming intoxicated who did not own that he was more or less a glutton; nor have I ever heard of a man who was a drunkard who was careful in his dietetic habits. All historical facts confirm this view. If you go back into that period of civilization known as the Middle Ages, and on to our own time, you will find in all places where drunkenness has prevailed, that there has existed with the drunkards, and with the population out of which drunkards are made, a gluttonous indulgence at table. The Norman Baron was a glutton; the Saxon Franklin was a glutton: the fat abbot was a glutton; the mitred priest was a glutton; the politician, statesman, merchant, who became a drunkard was a glutton. Wherever men drank, they feasted gluttonously. They ate to excess, and thus they drank to excess Had their habits of eating been corrected, their habits of drinking would have followed suit inevitably.

This is the history of drunkenness. It is connected with inordinate alimentiveness. Whenever a man begins to eat gluttonously, he creates for himself that appetitive desire for stimulants which it is next to impossible, and in most cases quite impossible, to control. Hence, it is important for those who are interested in having men and women sober, and so in full possession of their reason and all their higher faculties, to give heed to the matter of eating. Simple eating always leads to sobriety in respect to the use of stimulants, while highly seasoned food awakens the desire for stimulants, and thus creates an appetite which under social conditions favorable to indulgence is almost sure to upset all moral considerations, and leave the tempted and the tried to become victims. Our drunkards are not made in the saloons; they are simply graduated there. They take their initiation in their homes around their own tables. The father and the mother lay in themselves the foundation, and carry over to their children a constitutional liking for stimulants. This liking existing in the child as a tendency, is developed under the table arrangements into an actual appetite. So, from the eating of stimulating and exciting foods, affecting the nerves of the stomach, arises an irritable condiïuon of the nerves of nutrition, and by reflex action of the nerves of taste, and at length there is awakened a longing or desire for something to overcome the ·feeling of exhaustion, which, when stimulants are not in use, is always noticeable, and sometimes imperious in its demands.

It does not follow, however, that the appetite for strong drinks is attributable only to the irritation caused to the nerves of nutrition and taste by reason of the use of highly seasoned foods. Articles of diet which in themselves lack the constituents to make good the waste to which the nerve structures are subjected in performing their proper office, have a direct effect in awaking and producing the desire for stimulating beverages. This cannot be otherwise while the staple articles of food in use by our population at large are, many of them, defective in those properties out of which nerve structure can be built.

The nervous system in the human body is a wonderful organization. As the medium by which vital force is conserved and transmitted from the centers of the extremities of the nerve structure, it needs to be repaired by the use of appropriate nutrition just as much as do the muscles of the body. It is of the utmost importance that our muscles should be kept sound, full and effective. We are frightened if from any cause they shrink and shrivel. We never reason about an equal necessity on the part of the nervous system to repair and keep itself good. We eat to keep ourselves muscularly strong, not to keep ourselves nervously healthy, and thereby we suffer feebleness, loss of strength, loss of power of endurance, and expose ourselves to the incursions of a great variety of diseases. A man can wear away his nerves by activity, or from want of proper nutriment of them, as readily and decidedly and observably to the pathologist, as he can wear away his muscles; and when the nerves in the body, that ought to be in their full development as big as a doubled and twisted brown thread, come to be not larger than a hair, they can no longer perform their office. From want of this capacity a great many diseases marked by debility ensue.

Physicians make one great mistake in treating diseases of the nervous system. They administer stimulants and tonics in the vain hope to elaborate out of the reversed energy fresh supplies, when the truth is there are no supplies left; and where there are none in a man, stimulants, tonics, and nervines of every kind are contra-indicated, and if they are persistently administered, the patient dies. If, instead of these, nutriment to the nervous system were given, so that the nerves could be left to increase in size and be restored to vigor, their patients would get well. Lacking nutrients, but furnished with stimulants and excitants, still further exhaustion follows on their feebleness and they die.

Under a great variety of circumstances exhibited in our common life men feel a strong desire for stimulants. That desire grows out of the starved condition of the nerves in their bodies. Furnished with stimulants, this sense of starvation is overcome, and for the time a fictitious result is secured, which the

patient makes himself believe, and perhaps his physician is led to believe, may be substantially recuperative; but, like every other fallacy, this hope of his
rests on nothing, and so, in the end, the stimulants
and the tonics fail him. If you give to this debilitated, disordered, diseased, exhausted living body, by
way of ailment, the means of repairing its starved
nerve tissues, the desire for stimulants is lost.
Under the recuperative effect of nutrients the longing for stimulants disappears. While this is true of
a sick man whose disease is marked by nervous debility, it is just as true of an habitual drunkard.
Every drunkard is so by reason of the starved nerve
tissues in his body. This covers both classes of
drunkards—for we have two well defined and separ-
ate classes of inebriates—one, whose drunkenness is
a vice primarily, disease only laying in the distance;
the other, whose drunkenness is a disease primarily
with reflex tendencies therefrom to viciousness. But
whether it be your vicious or your sick drunkard, in
either case he is so because of the greatly disordered
diseased, debilitated nerve tissue.

It is now twenty-five years since I took the position
that drunkenness is a disease arising out of waste of
the nerve tissue, oftentimes finding the center of its
expression in the solar plexus or network of nerves
that lie behind the stomach, and reflecting itself to
the brain and spinal column by means of the great
Sympathetic. Since that time there have been under
my care not less than a hundred habitual drunkards,
some of them with such a desire for liquor that if
they could get it they would keep drunk all the time;
others have periodic turns of drunkardness, during

the paroxysms of which they would remain drunk for
a week or a fortnight at a time. Every one of these
persons was so far gone as to have lost self respect,
character and position, and many of them fine estates.
In only two instances have I failed to give back good
health and sobriety where these individuals have
been under my personal management and direction;
and of all the agencies that have been brought to
bear upon them, save the psychological, none have
proved so effectual as those of diet and bathing.

It is morally and physically impossible for any man
to remain a drunkard who can be induced to forego
the use of tobacco, tea, coffee, spicy condiments, common salt, flesh meats, and medicinal drugs. If his
diet consists of grains, fruits, and vegetables, simply
cooked, and keeps his skin clean, he cannot, for any
length of time, retain an appetite for strong drinks.
The desire dies out of him, and in its stead comes up
a disgust. This disgust is as decidedly moral as it is
physical. His better nature revolts at the thought
of drinking, and the power in him to resist is
strengthened thereby. The proof of this can be seen
at any time in our institution, where we have always
persons under treatment for inebriety. The testimony is ample, is uniform, is incontrovertible. The
patients themselves testify that they became sober,
not from any moral consideration at first operative
in them, but because under the plan of living to
which they were subjected the appetite died out; and
when a man grows away from a liking for any particular alcoholic drink, and has, beyond this, a dislike
for it spring up in him, it is quite improbable that he
will use it of his own accord; not very probable that

he will indulge in it at the suggestion of others.
Thus we readily see how effective for a restoration
to thorough health the dietetic department of our
common life may be made.

Children brought up only on milk and grains,
fruits and vegetables, simply cooked, leaving alone
flesh meats, condiments and stimulo-narcotic table
beverages, never become drunkards. The love for
simple food cultivated in childhood can never, under
any circumstances, be lost. When the child has
grown up his liking for simple foods is still active;
he prefers the grains, fruits, and vegetables. If he
has been fed during his early days on bread made of
unbolted wheat flour, the nerves of his body will
have been kept so healthy that no desire for stimulating drink will ever be awakened in him. I no not
believe that it is possible to awaken a desire for exciting liquors in a child, boy or man, who has never
eaten superfine flour, nor flesh meats, nor condiments. To awaken such an appetite he must resort
to the use of one or all of these substances. Keep
him away from them persistently, and leave him free
to follow his bent, and he will never resort to stimulants under any circumstances. However fatigued,
tired out or exhausted, the system calls for nourishment, not for excitement. If thirsty, the call is for
liquids which have nothing in them that is stimulating. Add to this that one of the greatest securities
against the development of an appetite for strong
drinks is the free use of fruits; and that you have in
the grains and the fruits eaten a thorough protection
against the desire for any stimulant.

It is not possible for a drunkard to eat unleavened

bread, made from unbolted wheat flour, and uncooked fruits such as the apple, pear, plum or apricot, or
any fruits growing in the temperate zone, and nothing else, for six months without having the desire
for liquor substantially die in him. Of course he
must not use medicines, drug poisons, tobacco, nor
spices. The simplicity of such a diet is thoroughly
restorative, and completely effectual to overcome his
longing for liquor. A child fed in this way is kept
from any uprisal of an appetite for strong drink.
His blood is healthy, and his nerves are well supplied
with proper constituents; his bones are strong; his
muscles sound, cordy and full, and his body being in
perfect health, the longing for strong drinks to make
good something lacking does not exist.

It seems a great pity that we go on by reason of a
bad system of dietetics making our children into
stimulant drinkers; making our young men dependent
on stimulants, to end their career at last as drunkards, while it is so easy to prevent this, and even to
recover those who have already fallen into this terrible debasement. I have found it impossible to cure
drunkards while I allowed them to use flesh meats.
I regard the use of flesh as laying right across the
way of restoration. Aside from its nutriment, it
contains some element or substance which so excites
the nervous system as in the long run to exhaust it,
to wear out its tissue, and render it incapable of natural action. In this condition of the system come
the reactions which are abnormal, and thence the
paroxysm of craving for liquor, which is so strong as
to overcome all moral restraints, obscure the judgment, enfeeble the will, and turn the man into a

creature having powerful desires with thoroughly aroused passions, and incapable of self control.

Every drunkard, therefore, who comes to us for treatment, takes his place in Our Home under these conditions: He must not be so far degraded as to have no desire to get well; if so, we connot take him, for we have no high walls, barred gates, padded rooms, nor any of the conditions of absolute restraint. He must consent to give up tobacco, tea, coffee, flesh meats of every kind, the contents of the castor, and common salt (I do not mean that he does this the first day he comes); and to the risk of whatever sickness that may ensue, without the use of any drug medicines. Matriculated on these terms, he can no more help becoming a sober man than water can help running down hill in a smooth unobstructed channel.

If, then, temperance men and women can be made to believe and understand that gluttony comes always before drunkenness, and will consent to operate in the prevention of drunkenness, and its cure on the basis of a sound and scientific system of dietetics, we may yet hope to see hundreds and thousands of youths—who otherwise must become drunkards or die early from the destructive effects of a "moderate" use of alcoholic poisons—stand up in the fullness of health, in the glory of their strength, in the enthusiasm of the largest expectations and prospects in life, to honor God in their day and generation, and to serve their fellow men.

Fruit and Old Age.

At a meeting of the National Food Society, of London, Drs. Emmet and Helen Densmore, stated among other things, that all men should and could live to be two hundred years old. That the prime of life should be from the eightieth to the hundredth year, and that, but for our blind disobedience of the laws governing nature, all humanity could complete a couple of centuries of existence upon this globe.

"I believe the time is coming," says Mrs. Densmore, on her recent visit to this country, "when it will be as great a disgrace to be ill as to be drunk. Intemperance in food has done as much to curse humanity as the abominable liquor habit.

Not only will proper food insure health, vigor and old age for man beyond twice the supposed natural span of life, but a woman's beauty may be enhanced, and the period of her youthful charms extended to four or five score years.

These attractive desideratums, however, are only to be obtained by a sweeping revolution in the common ethics of eating.

They do not hesitate to prophesy that all agriculture and cattle-breeding will gradually cease, and "no longer will the logical sequence of a cereal diet denude the earth of trees, but a food which involves the planting of orchards and the restoration of the earth to its natural beauty, will be the diet of the coming race."

The head and front of the "natural food" advocate's doctrine is that man is essentially a fruit-eater, and has merely by force of circumstances degenerated into the ranks of the carnivora.

If again he abjure flesh and confine himself, not to a vegetarian, but to a strictly frugivorian diet, it is claimed that his span of life would be more than doubled, and that sickness or ill-health would be unknown.

" Not only will the chemists and drug stores, so far as the preparation and sale of drugs and remedies are concerned, be done away with, but sending for a physician for any other purpose than for surgery will be unknown."

" It has been deducted from experiments made on soldiers, and with inmates of public institutions since the formation of our society, that for an average adult performing healthful, but not excessive labor, about twenty-one to twenty-two ounces of dried food in the twenty-four hours are requisite to keep up weight and strength. Of this, nearly seventeen ounces must be carbonaceous, or heat giving; about four ounces nitrogenous, or that which is intended for the support of the muscular action, and less than an ounce of the phosphatic, to support the brain or nervous system, and a small percentage of salts for the bony structure. All of these are found happily combined in fruit."

" If fruit be analyzed, it will be found that a large portion is carbonaceous like the starch in bread. In dried figs there is about 68 per cent. of glucose, or twice as much as in bread. Dates and bananas are similarly rich in this carbonaceous element."

The Vegetarian.

Volume I., attractively bound in linen, 236 pages, price $1.00

Contains many valuable articles on the subject and would make a suitable present for Vegetarians or thinking people.

THE PERFECT WAY IN DIET.

A treatise advocating a return to the natural and ancient food of our race.

—BY—

ANNA KINGSFORD,

Doctor of Medicine of the Faculty of Paris,

Sixth Edition, 1895. Price $1.00, Post Free.

THE VEGETARIAN PUBLISHING CO., 40 John St., New York.

THE VEGETARIAN·

SUBSCRIPTION :

Per Year, prepaid, to any part of the World, ... 25 cents.
10 Subscriptions, to different addresses . . . . . $1.00.
Single copies, 2 cents ; 50 cents per 100.

Published Monthly by
The Vegetarian Publishing Company, 40 John Street, New York City.

Entered at the New York Post Office as Second-class matter.

VOL. II. AUGUST 15, 1896. No. 2.

The Food for Students.

I have just read in the *New York Tribune* an abstract of your address entitled "University Education as a Foundation for Lifework." Among the many excellent suggestions which the address contains are two to which I take exception :—

"The scholar especially needs brawn as well as brain ; because, in order to be a scholar, he must pay the inevitable tax levied on every perpetual hard student ; and also because the supreme, practicable mental exertion which is the business of his life, is directly contingent on the fineness and fullness of his physical forces. Let the student, then, give earnest heed to the care and culture of his body. It is the home, the instrument, the mold, and the eternal companion of his soul. Let him know that sipping gruel and languidly lounging over books until his midnight lamp burns low, can never make him either a scholar or a man. Let him eat beef and mutton in generous slices."

Considered from any point of potential energy which food may be supposed to possess, beefsteak and mutton must necessarily, by reason of the elements that make them up, rank low. The best beefsteak has only about 38 per cent. of nutrition. This is only a little above the potato. It is therefore a food which, considered as aliment, is altogether untrustworthy; for no human body can long sustain itself in good health which has to eat a food as a staple two-thirds of which is made up of factitious or adventitious matters, having in them no power whatever to furnish material out of which blood can be made. If any man, therefore, were to eat only beefsteak for food he would either become a gluttonous eater, and in this direction become sensual and greatly debauched, or else fail in physical strength and become greatly enfeebled. Beefsteak, therefore, cannot rank beside the grains. The grain which we call wheat has 85 per cent. nutriment in it. This, compared with beefsteak, is more than as much again. One pound, therefore, of wheat will go more than twice as far as a pound of beefsteak.

But its deficiency in nutrition is not by any means its most objectionable feature when used as a staple food by the student. It has, in addition to whatever nutrient elements it contains, the quality of exciting the nervous system unduly, and so increasing the heart's action, and thus the rapidity with which all the vital processes are carried on. This is a very strong objection to its use by the student; for, if ever a human being is placed in conditions where, in order to accomplish the objects he seeks, he needs to be in the greatest composure, the whole life force working

organically and functionally with the least friction,
and so giving his mental faculties opportunity to exercise themselves without bodily reactionary disturb-
ances, a student needs it.

No student can eat beefsteak liberally or generously without having the habitual pulsations of the
heart ten beats higher in a minute than if he lived on
grains, vegetables and fruits, and who can estimate
the difference between a pulse at eighty or seventy
and between seventy-five and sixty-five in the accom-
plishments which a student will reach in a course of
years? For, to the degree that he is subject to rapid
expenditure of nervous force, will he be compelled
to undergo rapid changes of all the solid particles of
his body; and in the degree of this rapidity will
come, to a close and severe student, a conscious effort of the heart, and after a little a sense of cerebral
disquiet; then, by and by, a flitting before him of a
feeling of mental incompetency and restlessness of
spirit, and arousal of his passions, with accompany-
ing insubordination, and at last conviction that he
cannot command himself. Nothing is more detrimental to the mental faculties of any person than
unnecessarily rapid molecular changes in his body.
The slower, while at the same time the more equable,
the metamorphosis of tissue the surer is a person,
other things being equal, of large command of his
mental and moral faculties.

This aliment, having in it the quality to so affect the
brain and the nerve centers as to produce increased
action of the heart, increased action of the lungs,
rapid digestion, rapid disorganization of tissue, and
frequent call for evacuation of defecable material

that has been broken down and which needs to be cast out, is thus one of the worst kinds of food that a student can eat. The brain feels the effect and becomes excited by it. The ganglionic nervous system, as well as the sympathetic, also becomes affected by it. The quickening of the faculties and emotions which such persons undergo by reason of the new thoughts, new ideas, and enlarged association of ideas which study begets, becomes exhaustively intense, and therefore reaction against this exhaustion after a while either becomes impossible or ruinously destructive.

Such food, therefore, is not desirable for students, as it places their nervous system under constant stimulation. Now, in whatever form, stimulation is the last thing to which a student should be subjected. What if the stimulant were alcohol? Who would advise students to drink stimulating drinks generously? Thousands, who have been led to investigate the effect on brain tissue and nerve structure in general of drinking alcoholic liquors habitually, though in decided moderation, know that to drink any alcoholic mixture so that the animal spirits shall be in constant exhilaration, is only breaking down nerve power in a body to leave it all the sooner a wreck.

Now if this be true, as unquestionably it is, of alcoholic stimuli, why may not it be true of any substance whose ordinary, legitimate, and absolute effect is the same, though in a modified degree? Who can doubt that the conscious difference in effect upon a person's strength, either of body or mind, which beefsteak produces over good bread, is to be attributed to the stimulus which the beef contains, and which the bread does not contain, and not to any superiority in nutritive matter? If, then, to eat beefsteak is to be stimulated, it is to have evolved power for use, a re-supply of which the beefsteak does not at all contain, therefore making it an unreliable, unsubstantial, and unhealthy food for a student.

I have seen persons made thoroughly drunk by drinking—not very largely either—of warm beef blood. I have seen a woman, so enfeebled that she could not walk, eat a slice of rarely-cooked beefsteak, and within ten minutes rise from her bed, and, with as much apparent strength as one might ever need, walk a mile. Is it to be supposed for a moment that this person received such an amount of nutrition from it that within ten minutes after its being introduced into the stomach, the nerve structures, and through them the muscles whereby she was able thus to move off vigorously, were repaired? If this were not the case, she was affected by the stimulus of the food, and to be thus stimulated beyond the line of nutriment is always to be regretted except in cases of great emergency.

But there is another urgent reason why students should not use beefsteak. Under any college curriculum with which I am conversant, the student must, in the nature of the case, be largely of sedentary habits. Under such circumstances the excretions in his system must work off slowly. True, some advise much physical exercise, but I am sure that the brain work which one must do to win high standing in college contra-indicates a great amount of physical exercise. If, then, he has so much thinking and

learning to do that to stand high in his class he cannot devote time to boating, fishing, sporting, racing,
etc., then it is very desirable that he should eat nutrient food which is not stimulating. Because, if
stimulated, he *must* exercise, for, if he do not exercise, he will study *excitedly*, and this is always bad.

Again, the beefsteak of which students are advised
to eat generously is largely made from the flesh of
animals that have been stall-fed. The ox, though
sluggish in its constitution and slow in its motions,
has instinctively the disposition to roam, and, like
the buffalo on the western plains, if left to itself in
its grazing, will walk several miles in a day. This
exercise relieves the tissues of superabundant waste
material. Through kidneys and bowels, through
skin and lungs, the effete matters are carried off
under exercise. But what must be the condition of
an animal which is shut up in a stall, deprived of
exercise, and not infrequently of light, and made to
eat all that it possibly can? In a little while its system becomes plethoric; nature then recognizes the
new relation, and the kidneys and bowels act more
largely than before. Nevertheless, they cannot carry
off waste matters as fast as the accrete matters are
furnished, and so the animal begins to grow fat.
This fatness is made up largely of waste material
which under other circumstances would have been
cast out, and so lodges itself wherever there are adipose or fatty cells to hold it. It pushes itself in
between the fibers of the muscles, separating these,
and thus giving to them that quality which by meat-
eaters is called "tenderness." If these little layers
of fat were wanting, the fibers of the muscles would

be consolidated, and so by their compactness be made tough. This animal thus situated, when loaded with fat, is driven to the butcher's, killed, hung up, sold, cooked, and eaten, it may be, by students. It is considered excellent meat because it is full of venous blood and is tender in its fibers, they being kept apart by fat which has been deposited between them.

But what is the effect? He is stimulated by it, is rendered energetic; yet there is not a nerve structure in his body that will not suffer from this one excitable condition imposed upon it. Every vital organ suffers. His blood becomes debilitated and befouled. He has eaten the wasteage that the stall-fed ox, by reason of his confinement, could not exhale and excrete from his system; and do you commend a young man to eat generously of this food if he would succeed in life? Many a man, by eating this poisoned flesh-meat, so loved by the gourmand, so prized by gluttons, has laid the foundation of incurable disease, from which no medical skill could save him. Take away the use of fattened meats and you take away a predisposing and largely provoking cause of many of the diseases from which our college students die. But there is a better food, vastly better for students, an aliment that will furnish them with a support to the brain and the nervous structure, without inducing exhaustion; at the same time it will prevent exhaustion. I am not at all under the impression that students in our colleges and universities have too much work to do. A man's brain was made to work. It cannot last, however, if it works excitedly. It must work after law if it would remain healthy, and the law of this working demands that, if you put it to work you shall ensure repair; and when wear and repair are equal there need be no sickness nor long intervals of rest. Ten hours of close study, with two hours of bodily exercise and ten hours of sleep, is none too much for a human brain to stand, provided always that, for the material loss which it has to undergo by reason of its activities, there is at the same time material repair. This repair can only come through food of such a kind that, when converted into blood, can supply the material to the brain which has been used up. The very poorest food that a man can eat whereby the loss to his brain or to his nervous structure can be made good, is beefsteak. Analyse it and you will find it so. Its constituent elements are not what you can make good nerve structure out of. You can make muscle out of it, but muscular tissue and nervous tissue are two very different textures, and what will make the one will not make the other.

What, then, is the food which will supply the waste nervous tissue? It is wheat, good white wheat, ground whole into an unbolted flour and cooked in forms that are relishable to the taste, and yet so that the proximate elements of the grain shall not be changed. Then you have a food that will supply to the brain and to the nervous system all its losses caused by the operation of the mental faculties.

Of all the edibles, not one is at all to be compared in its completeness as a food for man with wheat. A human being can find in it, if he will not spoil it by preparation, but will use the whole of it—outer bark, inner rind, and central starchy pulp—constituent elements that will, in excellent measure, nourish every organ in the body. From the hair on his head to the nails on his feet there is not an organ so made up of substances that wheat will not supply the waste. In an eminent degree it is fitted to supply the material which the brain and nervous system need. In doing this it serves a most significant purpose. It preserves health by furnishing the various tissues with their complement of substance. It protects against disease because it keeps the nervous structure in high vigor. It is needful that this department of the physical organizations be kept in good repair, otherwise the nervous system becomes disordered, and then every other organ or class of organs in the body becomes affected.

Almost daily some man of note in this country dies of apoplexy or paralysis, or is smitten with epilepsy or softening of the brain. Scarce an hour passes but some man or woman dies untimely, dies in the dawning of adult life, dies in the very prime of life, dies just when the summit of life has been reached, dies of bilious fever, typhoid fever, dysentery, hemorrhage of the lungs, rheumatism of the heart, or some other accursed disease which has been induced by the long-continued use of foods which have starved the nervous structure, and thus deprived the individual of his divinely-appointed constitutional protection.

I do not reason thus without experience. In a twenty-five years' presidency of the largest hygienic institution in the world, I have had occasion to deal with thousands of men who have broken down either while preparing for college or while in college, or in the pursuits of life subsequent to graduation; and in the majority of these cases I have found them to be

men who, all their lives, had been advised to eat,
and had eaten largely, of flesh-meats. Nevertheless,
they had come to me with their nervous systems all
broken down, not from disease but from debility.
Their brains were worth but little for use, and their
spinal and sympathetic nerves were no better. The
organs of their bodies whose play, when in health,
produces the most delightful results, were all in disorder—stomach inert, liver torpid, kidneys congest-
ed, bowels constipated, skin dry and harsh, heart
palpitating, lungs weak, brain useless. They had
tried many remedies of many physicians "and were
nothing bettered but rather made worse." By
changing their dietetic habits, taking off pressure
from one part and putting it on to another, slowly,
steadily, surely they came back to health, and now
for years the major part of them has been hard at
work, fresher and better as the years go on, living
without meat, living on grains, fruits and vegetables.
There is a whole system of divine philosophy in this
matter of eating food which nutrifies the body without exhausting it.

The ordinary movements which a student instinctively takes—and in this direction instinct is, and in
many other directions might be, of great service—
will supply his bodily structure with the nutritive
energy which his muscular organism demands for
healthful ends. He is not called upon to make physical exercise a duty, unless from faulty conditions of
living in other ways, and especially in matters of
eating, he makes his body plethoric with waste matters. Even then philosophy will not justify as an
abstract proposition the plan and method you sug-

gest. It only defends it on the basis of expediency. The true method for the student is to live so simple, yet nutritively, that severe strain of muscle is not required to secure restoration of tissue or the thorough excretion of it from the body.

Living thus simply, all the organic processes, whether ending in waste or repair, will be carried on so quietly yet so effectively, as to demand a *minimum* of muscularity. In such conditions the student has at use all the vital energy which his constitutional capabilities can furnish, and he has it at avail. Put such a person to study and he takes delight in it— tire him, and rest refreshes him. He needs food which, when made into blood, will build up brain and nerves and fill him with nerve force. For this end the flesh of the ox is not at all to be compared to the flour made out of the entire grain of wheat.

Third Hand Food.

Vegetarians are apt to refer to the flesh of animals as second hand food, that is, vegetable matter that has been eaten by cattle and after being converted into flesh is taken second hand (or stomach) as food for man, but according to an announcement of a Philadelphia company sent us by Mr. R. Hecker of that city the public are now to take their nourishment at third hand. Not content with feeding cows on distillery slops it is now proposed to make the poor animals cannibals like their owners and feed them on the ground bodies of dead horses, etc.. so as to fatten them quickly and provide *delicate food* for the consumption of man.

Ammonite or Prepared Offal.

"There are establishments in Philadelphia and other Eastern cities where slaughter house offal and recently dead animals are worked into food for living animals. The raw material is first cut up and passed through a machine which tears it into shreds. It is then boiled in benzine in a closed iron cauldron, resulting in a dry mass weighing about one-fifth of the original bulk. These establishments pay for fresh carcasses of dead hogs *twenty-five* to *fifty cents* each, cattle *fifty cents* to *$1*, horses *$8* to *$12*. This material called ammonite (from ammonia), contains in the most available state all the elements needed for forming the tissues of the living animal. Hence, when fed to the growing or fattening animal, the process of growth is rapidly accelerated. The day is not far distant when this well established scientific principle will be turned to more general use in this country."

Prunes and Figs.

We learn from the San Francisco papers, that a man in Oakland, with his family, are living entirely on the above fruits, one meal a day and no change. His intelligent flesh-eating neighbors probably thought his simple diet was a reflection on their own bestiality and called in the agents of the Society for Prevention of Cruelty to Children who thoroughly investigated the case. They found that the eldest daughter had attained her majority; the society could not do anything, and the other children were thriving on the diet of figs and prunes and were as healthy and fat as anyone could wish; nothing could be done for them.

Mr. Henry Krause, who is a widower, stoutly defended his right to diet his children as suited his fancy, he admitted that the bill of fare was always the same, and that his children partook of but one meal per day.

It is truly a wonderful revelation to Christians to find that it is possible to subsist on the food which their religion teaches them was created for their sole sustenance.

The Food for Strength.

The splendid achievements of vegetarian athletes is gradually turning the attention of professional strong men to their mode of diet and we learn from our English contemporaries that the vegetarian restaurants in London are crowded with cyclists, runners, swimmers, etc. From what I have noticed I think that few indeed are strict vegetarians, but that the variety of courses on the unspeakable menu card is the attraction. Here is what Mr. James Parsley, of the Surrey Wheelers and Vegetarian C.C., says: "Of course you know I am a vegetarian. I have been so for over twelve months, and I find the diet agrees with me, and I have improved wonderfully." This Surrey amateur is well known to cyclists as a great hill-climber, and as the victor in the recent Catford up-hill struggle. These contests have, by the way, been held up such hills as Westerham, Brasted, Titsey and Toys. Mr. Parsley was second last year when the Catford event was held at Westerham, but he won the handicap. This year at Toys-hill he reversed his position, being first in scratch race and second in handicap. At Cheltenham last year he rode second from scratch in a hill climb. He has won several speed events, and still holds the tricycle record from London to Brighton and back of 3 hours 18 min. 28 sec. and it is his intention to go for records on a single in the near future.

Parsley was born in Bristol twenty-four years ago, is five feet eight inches in height, and weighs when stripped ten stone six pounds. He believes in quiet spins along the country roads as a means of obtaining condition.

New South Wales Vegetarian Society Annual Meeting.

The Executive in presenting their report for the year, have pleasure in stating that debates have been held with various Literary and Debating Societies in city and suburbs, and although not so frequent as they would wish, there is good reason to believe the subject of the debates has been well received. Several lectures have been given by Pastor Corliss, Dr. Kellogg and Mr. D. Lacy, in which the subject of food reform has been well treated and discussed. In September, last year, Mrs. Annie Besant being in Sydney, and as she was known to be in full sympathy with the work of the Society a deputation of members waited upon her and presented her with a very neat address in accepting which, she expressed herself

decidedly in favor of a non-flesh diet; a full report of
her remarks appeared in the daily press.

JAMES W. LAWTON, *Hon. Sec.*

The fourth anniversary of the formation of the
New South Wales Vegetarian Society was celebrated
by a banquet at the Waratah Tea rooms, Pitt street,
which was attended by a large number of members
and friends. The menu was composed entirely of
vegetarian dishes, excellently prepared followed by a
variety of sweets and fruits. Mr. F. H. Satchell,
president of the society, in the unavoidable absence
of the Mayor, occupied the chair, and, at the conclusion of the report, he spoke of the advantages of
vegetarianism over the commonly accepted dietary.
It was a mistake, he said, to think that vegetarians
lived solely on potatoes and cabbage. Their dietary
covered a much wider area, and included not only
vegetables, but all the cereals and every variety of
fruit, as well as tea, coffee and milk. He repudiated
the idea that by eliminating flesh-meat from their
dietary men lost energy and mental force, and held
that the experience of all vegetarians conclusively
proved the contrary. But while they did not go so
far as to contend that men could not keep in health
and strength on flesh diet, they did hold that meat
was not essential to health and strength. Their personal records showed that vegetarians were healthier
than meat-eaters, as, among other advantages, they
ran none of the risks inseparable from the eating of
flesh-meat, which was notoriously a common vehicle
of disease, a danger from which the vegetarian dietary was wholly free. The remainder of the evening was spent in social fashion, musical contributions
being rendered by Mrs. Baker, Misses Wright and
Louden, and Mr. Massey.

THE VEGETARIAN·

SUBSCRIPTION:

Per Year, prepaid, to any part of the World, ... 25 cents.
10 Subscriptions, to different addresses . . . . . $1.00.
Single copies, 2 cents; 50 cents per 100.

Published Monthly by
The Vegetarian Publishing Company, 40 John Street, New York City.

Entered at the New York Post Office as Second-class matter.

VOL. II.   SEPTEMBER 15, 1896.   NO.. 3

Flesh Eating and Disease.

BY THE LATE W. GIBSON WARD, F.R.H.S.

What relation has a particular diet to disease? The present writer has had wide experience in the matter and brings facts which he knows to the full glare of public opinion.

First, there is epilepsy—a most fearful malady. To see a poor sufferer struggling with every limb and foaming at the mouth, and possibly, if due care is not taken, biting through his tongue, involving severe suffering for a long period, is sad enough— still worse to see the gradual break down of body and mind ending in death.

According to the report of the Registrar-General, epilepsy caused 2,853 deaths in the year 1876, exactly 445 more than smallpox caused in that year. Except congenital cases, and a very few others, the *sequela* of some severe disease, these are all the consequences of a flesh diet. Dr. Lambe, an eminent London physician, some seventy years ago published the statement that in every case of epilepsy, not congenital, the patient had only to cease eating flesh of every sort and drink pure or distilled water and the evil should cease at once. So we have invariably found it.

Three cases which lately presented themselves were immediately cured. A Nottingham manufacturer wrote to me: "I have a daughter twenty-seven years old, apparently a healthy woman with a ruddy countenance, who for the last seven years has been fearfully afflicted with epileptic fits. She had been in London last year (1877) for eight months under the care of ——, but—as in all previous attempts— medical assistance has not been of the least benefit. This morning I met Mr. ——, and he wished me to write to you. If you can only give me a ray of hope you will confer, etc., etc." The reply was decisive and consolatory: "She shall never have another fit of epilepsy if you only withdraw all flesh food, and give her at first a careful vegetable diet, as laid down here, and pure water." As in every other case, the cure was immediate and final. Many similar cases could be detailed, but they all present the same testimony—instant relief, and no more fits. In one instance a severe sufferer said he had all the usual feelings before a fit, and felt certain one was coming on, and feared that the remedy, then followed only a few days, was likely to fail; but the symptoms gradually passed away, and he never had another fit. How trivial all cleansing of sewers seems, then, to the cleasing of stomach and veins and "the dome of thought " from the filth of the slaughter-house!

Then, again, paralysis, which carries off the fearful number of 11,934 persons, seems to be subdued in the same manner. There is the historical case of Dr. Adam Ferguson. It is detailed in Watson's " Practice of Physic," and in the preface of one of Sir Walter Scott's novels. The doctor, at sixty-five years of age, when lecturing to his class, was seized with paralysis. He was carried home by his students. He then sent for his friends, Dr. Back, the chemist (not a doctor of medicine, or his fate might have been sealed). " Turn a Pythagorean, man," were the words of his friend. He did turn Vegetarian at once. He recovered the use of his limbs and of all his faculties, and lived a hale and hearty vegetarian for thirty years afterwards. Sir Walter Scott says that his venerable appearance, his affected plain dress, and his ruddy health, put him in mind of a Flemish peasant.

We will next call attention to scarlet fever. In a report that we have just read of a severe outbreak of scarlet fever the dampness of the house was pointed out as the originating cause. Of course dampness is a great evil, but it had about as much to do with originating an attack of scarlet fever as it had to do with the crash of the Glasgow City Bank. The result of a poison which arises directly from the vile habits of society, it killed 16,893 persons in 1876, the last return that we have—more than sevenfold the mortality from smallpox from this one crime of the evil habits of English life. What a mockery is the visit of the Inspector of Nuisances, whose nose and eyes are not offended when the direst evil in relation to

disease is not seen or smelt or within his intelligence,
and even not in the least under his power!

It is not easy, indeed scarcely possible, to exag-
gerate the fearful effects of rheumatism. It is
credited in the Registrar's Report (for 1876) with
killing 3,640 human beings; but these figures, large
as they are, are but a trifle to the whole sum of the
evil. Heart disease kills 30,481, and beyond con-
troversy, rheumatism and its allied evil, gout, produce two-thirds of these deaths. Certainly these
25,000 deaths at least, are the result of the fearfully
erroneous diet of Englishmen. The origin of rheumatism is as obscure to most people as is the origin
of scarlet fever.

There is a ready, though delusive, excuse for rheumatism, rheumatic fever, and rheumatic arthritis.
It is attributed to wet, or damp, or to a cold. Now
neither wettings, nor dampness, nor a cold can produce rheumatic fever or rheumatic sufferings. The
blood must first be acid. Nature struggles with the
evil, and throws off the acid with the perspiration,
which is strong enough to dissolve gold, as the black
mark on a lady's neck under her gold chain testifies.
But at last a chill comes from a wetting, or a rush-
ing from a heated room and standing or riding in the
air at a low temperature, and there is no escape for
the acid from the blood, and then a fever burns
within, and probably a weakness is set up that nothing
ever removes.

Acid blood, then, is the origin and sustaining cause
of all rheumatic affections. But what produces it?
Unnatural and improper diet. Go to the shambles
and apply a bit of test paper to the juice of the flesh

there, and **you** find it gives an acid reaction, if you cannot gather grapes from thistles you are not likely to get alkaline blood from food which in its organic or inorganic state gives an excess of acids.

Vegetables and fruits of all kinds give more or less an excess of alkalies. People who are content with "the herb bearing seed and the tree producing fruit" for their diet cannot have rheumatic pains, or fevers, or their joints cemented together as in rheumatic arthritis. The evil result of acid blood, as manifested in other diseases—in leprosy and scurvy, for instance —we cannot detail here.

In our advocacy of natural diet—of Vegetarianism as the only dietary divinely prescribed for us— we are sometimes met with the argument that our Anglo-Saxon forefathers ate more flesh than we do; that indeed they lived nearly wholly on beef and beer; that the practice was continued during many centuries; that the maids of honor to Queen Elizabeth, and even the Queen herself, breakfasted on beefsteaks and beer.

Undoubtedly our Anglo-Saxon forefathers were a coarse people, almost devoid of refinement and literature, and given to riotous eating of flesh and drunken habits. That similarly debased habits were common in the reign of Elizabeth we must admit. But a change had for sometime been working, which dispensed with the necessity of living about half the year on salt meat, and which, by the introduction of salads and some other garden vegetables, to supply those alkalies to the blood without which healthy life is impossible, enabled them to escape some of the evils of a flesh diet.

We candidly admit that if it could be shown that the early English—living as they did almost wholly on flesh and beer—were as healthy as the people before them, the Britons and the Romans, or as our population of to-day, then our Vegetarian arguments would be useless or fallacious, and our notions of correct diet be quite absurd. But a knowledge of the sufferings of these beef-eaters and beer-drinkers, of the plague that never left them while they lived on salted flesh, with few or no vegetables, and drank beer freely (for really beer then, with a nearly exclusive diet of salted and fresh flesh meat, was a greater evil than it is now to any one who can keep his blood alkaline with vegetables) would appal the flesh eater, and confirm the arguments of the Vegetarian.

The Romans were an abstemious people.* We search their teachings on agriculture in vain to find a single allusion to stall-fed cattle for human food. Oxen were beasts of burden. They ploughed the land, and the ploughman thought as little of eating their toiling partners as of eating their harness or implements. We read of rich people having aviaries, that they could now and then eat a small but fat bird, and fish ponds to occasionally vary their diet with fish; but the mass of the people were practically Vegetarians, and gloried in vegetables. So much was this the case that the aristocratic families were named from vetches, beans, and other such viands. The Romans were in consequence a healthy

---

* The Romans. *i. e.*, the early Romans. The case was widely different at a later age, as Queen Boadicea seems to imply. The former was the age of Roman vigor; the latter of Roman decay.

people. When we dig up the remains of their druggists' shops, or houses of medical men, we find that doctors and quacks had nostrums to cure eye diseases, but scarcely anything else.

Our British people whom they invaded were too an abstemious people. Cæsar tells us that the Britons had a great variety of poultry, but that they never ate them, and only bred them for amusement and for their eggs. Then we have that brave British Queen Boadicea, or Bonduca, who harangued her troops and aroused their courage against the Romans. " Every bush," she said, "gives us food and every brook drink, but these Romans require cooked food and houses to live in," etc. A British grave was opened some years ago, and a mass of seeds was found where the stomach had been. They were the seeds of the wild raspberry. So that this early Briton had made his dinner off the bushes, and had been killed before he had digested the fruit. But that the Jutes, Angles, and Saxons who invaded our coasts and settled on our soil fed as coarsely as savages is nearly or quite true, and they suffered fearfully from disease in consequence. They filled the country with suffering, and made in every solitary spot a lazar-house. Among them the pestilence was not occasional, but constant. So it continued on through the Norman invasion, and even after they had become English, from throne to cottage, and only declined as vegetables became a large proportion of their daily food.

Many imagine leprosy to be some obscure disease alluded to only in the Bible. Leprosy was also a disease of the Middle Ages, more widely spread and more fearful in its results than any other in ancient or modern times. It is probable that the worst form of leprosy in early Jewish history was that now known as *elephantiasis*. The milder form of Jewish leprosy, called *bohak*, was neither severe nor contagious.

Leprosy in England and Europe arose gradually after the destruction of the Roman Empire as fast as barbarism spread with its uncleanness of personal habits, and its resort to animal food and beer as nearly exclusive articles of daily diet. In all ancient towns it was early found necessary to erect hospitals, and retreats, and churches, for those afflicted with leprosy. We have in England now hospitals built for lepers so ancient that their origin is unknown, such as the St. Bartholomew Hospital at Gloucester, and others. It is known that there were at least 9,000 hospitals in Europe for leprosy alone. Louis VII. of France left legacies to over 2,000 hospitals for lepers in his country. We have extant a touching account of a knight of vast wealth and influence, named Amiloun, expelled from his castle to be a beggar, almost in sight of his vast possessions and stately home; for the Normans in France virtually outlawed, as well as expelled from their homes, all lepers, and, as soon as their influence was established in England, they extended their sanitary measures and benevolent enterprise to lepers.

Hugo, or Eudo Dapifer—the steward for William the Conqueror—having received from him vast possessions in land in Essex, built, or rebuilt, and endowed a St. Mary Magdalen Hospital for lepers in Colchester. The hospital for lepers, dedicated to the same saint in the city of Exeter, is of unknown antiquity. Bartholomew, bishop of that city and diocese (1161-1184), finding its usefulness limited for want of funds, and the suffering of lepers unlimited, endowed it with considerable wealth. Pope Celestine III. granted or confirmed a charter in the year 1192, and the charity exists to this day.

Hubert, Archbishop of Canterbury, held a synod at Westminster, in the year 1200, to carry out the decree of the Council of Lateran (1172) to build a number of churches solely for leprous people, for they had long been expelled from all parish churches. They were to have priests, officers and graveyards exclusively for themselves. They were released at the same time from all claims for titles for their land or cattle. So careful and determined were our ancestors to remove from sight and smell every leper that a law was early in existence to enforce their removal out of towns and villages "to a solitary place." The writ is in our ancient law-books, entitled *De Lepaoso Amovendo*, and it is fully stated by Judge Fitz-Herbert in his *Natura Brevium*. King Edward III., finding that in spite of the old law leprous persons were concealed in houses inhabited by other persons, gave command to the Lord Mayor and Sheriffs to make proclamation in every ward of the city and its suburbs "that all *leprous* persons inhabiting there should avoid within fifteen days next," etc., etc.

At the city of Bath, a bath, with physicians and attendants, was provided and endowed exclusively for lepers—and the endowments are still paid. That the bath was occasionally efficacious, in connection with improved diet, we have sure evidence; for one leper in late days had fixed to the bath a mural tablet to say that "William Berry, of Garthorpe, near Melton Mowbray, in the county of Leicester, was cured of a dry leprosy by the help of God and the bath. 1737."

The simple fact of the introduction of the growth of vegetables into our islands was sufficient to do for the people what all the art of the doctors could not do —improve their health and remove pestilence from amongst them. If we read the ancient Chronicles of Island we find that beer and flesh meat were the only viands named and commended. Indeed, the *bo aire* was honored the most who had the largest kettle to boil flesh and the largest brewing apparatus.

In England it was much the same—beef and beer and bread were the three staples of human food. It was not until the end of the reign of Henry VIII. that any salads, carrots, turnips, or other edible roots were produced in England. The wealthy had imported vegetables before then from Holland and Flanders. Queen Catharine, when she wanted a salad, was obliged to send for it, by special messenger to the Continent. By a statute made in the reign of Henry VIII. *beef* and *pork* were to be sold at a half-penny a pound, *mutton* and *veal* at a half-farthing extra per pound. Butchers were compelled to sell at these prices between October 24 and the nativity of St. John. The custom of salting meat before the festival of St. Martin (November 11), for winter and spring consumption, was universal amongst all classes in our islands and over the Continent of Europe. One fact illustrates the custom and its supposed necessity: Thomas Williamson, of the county of Cumberland, who died in 1674, left certain lands, the rents of which forever were to be bestowed on the poor, "in *mutton* or *veal* at Martinmas yearly, when flesh might be bought cheapest, to be by them *pickled*, or *hung up* and dried, that they might have something to keep them within doors on stormy days.". The farmers then, having no roots or clover, could fodder through the winter only a small stock of cattle, so late calves and weakly yearlings and surplus stock of all sorts were sent to markets, fairs, and butchers, and sold for what they would bring.

The English people then, in common with all others on the Continent of Europe, lived for the greatest part of the year on salted flesh, with scarcely any vegetables. Their blood was thus deprived of the necessary alkali—the vehicle for conveying oxygen to purify it, and to burn up the carbonaceous materials of the food, and deprived likewise of the material that excludes from the venous system the excess of lactates of lime, etc.; so that nearly every power given to the blood by nature to keep man healthy was destroyed, or put aside by man himself to please his depraved appetite, or from want of knowledge or industry to cultivate garden vegetables.

Thus, merely approaching the teaching of Nature, in relation to the true diet of man, cleansed England and Europe of leprosy. Extend the good diet in the line of Nature's teaching—let man feed only on the diet his constitution was made for—and then, with due cleanliness of skin and other surroundings, smallpox could no more afflict mankind. Likewise rheumatism, rheumatic fevers, rheumatic arthritis, and bladder diseases, and many other evil visitations, would no more afflict humanity if exclusively vegetable diet were generally partaken. Thus also the whole of the ailments that follow necessarily on acid blood and the presence of various lactates soluble in such acid blood would be cut off. For no Vegetarian living fairly on fruits and green vegetables and potatoes, with the ground seeds of the cereals and ground or unground pulse, can have acid blood, nor can he therefore have rheumatic affections, or any disease depending on like conditions.

Such are a few of the evils of an unnatural diet. Now for thine own sake and the welfare and prosperity of all people, attend, O reader, and bend thy mind and appetite to nature and truth, for they are "the brightness of the everlasting light, the unspotted mirror of the power of God and the image of His goodness."—*Extracts from his writings published in various papers.*

Sport or Crime.

We have received permission to publish the following letter, written by a well-known Vegetarian to a niece and nephew spending a vacation in the mountains. If all children were blessed with relatives who would instruct them in the ways of peace and virtue instead of crime and bloodthirstiness there would be less acts of violence and murders for our criminal courts to investigate.—ED.

New York, August 13, 1896.

My Dear Walter and Ellie:—Just received your letters from your Sullivan County mountain resort. Amidst the sweltering heat of the city the letter heading in itself seems like a fresh whiff of mountain air.

I would have to lie, however, if I stated that your letters gave me any pleasure. The feeling they created was rather a painful one, especially, Walter's, who reports fishing as his favorite sport and amusement, in which torturing and killing, you, my dear Ellie, intend to take a part. Having now and then, with repugnant shuddering, watched the process of fishing, I observed that first a living earth worm (whose usefulness is greater than any other creature, man included, inasmuch as it furrows the earth for irrigation and the reception of seeds), is while yet alive torn to pieces, its quivering flesh fastened to a hook, then thrown into the water to entice a fish to its death. After hooking the bait in its mouth the bleeding and tortured fish is snatched out of its element, dashed on a stone or earth and left there bleeding and struggling until death ends its agony, And that is what you call great fun!

I could find some excuse for such savage bloodthirsty proceeding if it was a matter of starvation, you being the stronger, killing the weaker animal in order to continue your existence. But knowing you housed in that fashionable mountain hotel your indulgence in that savage sport is simply for pastime. I think I hear your answer, that the fish and the worm have to die, anyway, sooner or later. Very true. And in the frightful heat we are having in

New York just at present thousands of the little children of the poor in the closely packed tenement houses are also doomed to die for want of air and comfort. But what opinion would you have of me, if I wrote you that in order to have some pleasant pastime, fun and sport I was sallying forth, under cover of darkness, in these districts, and, baiting a little tot with a piece of candy, would suddenly thrust a sharp hook down its throat and enjoy its painful gasping and wriggling death struggle until it falls dying on the pavement ?

Would you address me then " My Dear Uncle," or would you not rather feel justified in addressing me " You vile murderer ?"

What pitiful and miserable beings are you, any-way, that in going to such a beautiful mountain place for recreation you cannot find it in any other way than by scattering torture and destruction among other creatures, who enjoy their existence perhaps as much or even more so than you do your own.

Do you know, Ellie, why that deer you mentioned getting a glimpse of in the woods ran away ? There was no other creature around to frighten it away, but recognizing you as a member of the human family, however small, it thought that you might have one of those death-dealing machines, a gun, and delight in taking its life, just for the fun of it. In Central Park, you are aware, these graceful creatures have no shyness, but come right close to lick our hands, their big melting eyes expressive with gratitude for a piece of cake or a peanut. In that place at least they need not fear our savage instinct.

Much thanks for your kind invitation to come up and spend a few days. As much as I should like the place, I am afraid we would see very little of each other. Having all the year received more than enough of dandyfied city folks, I should visit the farmers and watch their work, roam like Tom through the woods and mountains, but singing instead of barking, and observe with delight the great variety and richness of animal and plant life, of which we are ignorant, dwelling in cities. I had recently a few such delightful days and experienced some funny incidents in a little tramping tour in the Catskills.

You call yourself a great swimmer, Walter, my boy, don't you? How does this strike you? Yesterday I swam across the Hudson from the foot of 158th street to Jersey shore. About midstream I encountered some strong current which carried me almost to Pleasant Valley, then came a change of tide which forced me up to Fort Lee. I swam continuously about three and a half miles in about one hour, and just felt a little tired touching the Jersey shore side. The friend in the boat who piloted me across felt that only a big beefsteak could satisfy his exertion in sculling and could not help wondering that a supper of two cheese sandwiches and a glass of milk on top of a light breakfast in the morning could satisfy the exertion on my part.

With kindliest regards for all, yours forever, as ever affectionate uncle,

GEO. BRUNSWICK.

The Vegetarian.

Volume I., attractively bound in linen, 236 pages, price $1.00

Contains many valuable articles on the subject and would make a suitable present for Vegetarians or thinking people.

THE PERFECT WAY IN DIET.

A treatise advocating a return to the natural and ancient food of our race.

—BY—

ANNA KINGSFORD,

Doctor of Medicine of the Faculty of Paris,

Sixth Edition, 1895.   Price $1.00, Post Free.

THE VEGETARIAN PUBLISHING CO., 40 John St., New York.

THE VEGETARIAN·

SUBSCRIPTION:

Per Year, prepaid, to any part of the World, ... 25 cents.
10 Subscriptions, to different addresses . . . . . . $1.00.
Single copies, 2 cents; 50 cents per 100.

Published Monthly by
The Vegetarian Publishing Company, 40 John Street, New York City.

Entered at the New York Post Office as Second-class matter.

VOL. II.   OCTOBER 15, 1896.   No. 4.

Kill Not At All.

All reforms are of slow growth, and those requiring self denial of their advocates instead of offering aggrandizement, certainly do not have their pace accelerated thereby. If we preached self indulgence and promised immunity from the penalties imposed by the laws of nature on all who violate her laws, vegetarians would be numbered by the million instead of the thousand. The only reform which achieved immediate success was that inaugurated by Mahomet, and whatever we may think of Mahometanism at the present day, it was undoubtedly a great advance over the systems it overthrew at the commencement. Mahomet offered his followers the wealth of the heathens they destroyed and the immediate delights of a sensual paradise to those who fell in the attempt. No wonder that the advance was rapid and has continued and will continue to advance so long as any uncivilized people remain on earth.

Jesus Christ preached a religion of self-sacrifice, of love instead of hate, of humility instead of glory; teaching his followers to love instead of hate their enemies. The advance was correspondingly slow, and the greater part of the progress was owing to his followers living their own savage lives while professing his religion. And it is only after nearly nineteen hundred years that people in a sort of tentative way are beginning to believe what they have always preached; that it is a crime to kill. We presume the majority of the people always believed that it was wrong to kill their friends or even their fellow countrymen for gain, but of course this did not include privileged people, kings and princes, who, until the last hundred years or so, varying slightly in different countries, always had the prerogative of killing their inferiors, with or without cause, and killing one another, provided certain rules were carried out and formalities observed. But war, glorious war, covered by the name of patriotism, still retains its place in the affections and the hearts of the multitude, even though the people have been cheated by their rulers out of their just share of the proceeds. In old times all men were about equal at the game; none had special advantages except in brute strength and ferocity. Every man starting out in the ranks had the chance of returning a leader, that is, provided he was sufficiently bloodthirsty and was fortunate enough to save his life; but more than this, in the good old days every soldier had the pleasure of seeing the men he murdered and stealing their property. This is all changed now; the leaders have been studying since boyhood the trade of murder, and have acquired such advantages in this line that the private has no chance to catch up. Then, although he kills wholesale, the private is deprived of all the pleasure of his villainous trade and does not often get the chance of seeing the men he murders. And as for plunder, he would be punished if he stole a cent; his employers take it all. While in addition to all this, his chance of getting killed himself is steadily increasing. No wonder that the murder trade is not as popular as it used to be.

The best men in all civilized countries are beginning to talk of arbitration as a better way of settling international difficulties, and the best newspapers are deprecating the efforts of the unthinking who are doing their best to keep up the bloody ideas of the past. The *Evening Post* of October 6, writes as follows in an editorial.

". . . the delight the animal man takes in killing members of his own species on a great scale. In fact, since the dawn of civilization there is no art to the cultivation of which he has devoted as much time and money as the art of killing his own fellow-creatures wholesale. No other animal has shown the smallest disposition in that direction. There is nothing wonderful in the "bloodthirst" as displayed in the massacres of the Albigenses, the massacres in most Oriental wars after victory, massacres following a successful assault, or massacres on account of religion, like those in Turkey, when we have to-day millions of men in the most civilized parts of the world spending some of their golden years learning to kill their fellowmen dexterously and effectively.

Nay, the legislation among us all over the country in favor of hoisting flags over school houses was generally intended to inspire in the children a desire to kill in settlement of international disputes, and respect for the killing art.

There has not been in the history of philology anything so wonderful as the way in which the term "war" has been successful in disguising what the term designates. War is really one of the most shocking, barbarizing and brutal scenes in which man is the actor, but the term has been successful in representing it as simply a heroic sacrifice on behalf of one's country, in turning attention away from the man who kills to the man who is killed, from the power which attacks to the power which defends itself, and in concealing completely the awful misery inflicted on the non-combatants and the great destruction of property. No operations of lion, or tiger, or wolf, or hyena approach it in atrocity. Moreover, in all descriptions, scientific and other, of man as an animal, this love of killing his fellows is never alluded to, although it is his most marked peculiarity. If an individual, in fact, for any purpose acted in civil life as a warrior acts on the field, he would be considered a wretch unworthy to live, an enemy of the human race, but saying he did it in "war" is a complete answer to all criticism."

There is nothing new in these facts; every thinking man has argued it out in his own mind and then put it aside declaring that while the rest of the world is so savage we must keep up with the times in which we live and be prepared for the worst. This may be sensible, but it will never make men one whit better. The only way to improve mankind is to commence at once and to commence at the bottom; absolutely refuse to kill or to be implicated with those who do. Kill not at all, neither animals or man, either for malice or gain, for private enmity or public good, and above all do not pol'···'. yourself by eating the dead bodies of the slain.

A Vegetarian Athlete.

Morin, the wonderful French racing man, who disappointed five hundred American "rooters" for John S. Johnson when the Minneapolis rider met him in Paris, is trained by a physician. Morin has captured the Grand Prix two years in succession. This is pretty good evidence that his physician is useful to him. In an article on training, Morin's physician says:

"One can scarcely imagine how contrary the actual rules of training are to the laws of hygiene. This contrariety is due entirely to the views of the manager. What a mistake, for instance, to make young men eat rare meat, such as cutlets, beefsteak, mutton, etc., for the purpose of increasing their strength. There is nothing more opposed to the teachings of physiology. Notice the beasts of draught and burden, the horse and the ox, for example: they do the most exhausting muscular work, and have no need of flesh. Vegetables are much better than meat for the racing men. Again, even in observing the strictest rules of hygiene, training ought to be moderate. That is the way to remain a long time in the field and escape the fate of the champions of the past, who could not battle three successive years. The body of a rider is a locomotive, but an infinitely sensitive locomotive. If you heat it too much, if you burn too much coal, it explodes."

Some of the circuit chasers in this country who expect to enjoy themselves after each contest, and have an idea that they will be able to keep up the pace indefinitely, will be interested in Morin's case.

The Advance of Civilization.

At various times we have stated that flesh-eating man is a natural murderer, and only fear of the consequences prevents his killing his fellow citizens.

The following extract from the New York *Sun*, fully bears out our assertion.

". . . Lieut. Leist, a German official in the Cameroons. . . ."

"He had taken advantage of the almost unlimited power conferred on him and of the fact that he was so far from the restraints of civilization, and he had been guilty of the most unspeakable atrocities toward the native population. For the slightest offences the natives were flogged in a manner that would have been unpardonable had they been the greatest criminals. A hippopotamus whip was always used, and if the poor creature survived his punishment it was a miracle.

"The chief indignities, however, were heaped upon the women. Regarded as little higher than animals, they were not even treated with the respect due human beings, much less creatures of the gentler sex. One of the favorite amusements of the officers in Leist's following, was to form a circle about a group of native girls and force them, with the lash if necessary, to dance naked in their presence. Complete exposure of such facts was made in the court of justice at Potsdam, before which Leist was arraigned. Public feeling ran high on the subject, but Leist was merely cashiered, though his crimes deserved a severer penalty.

"To us Americans in Germany the most interesting feature of the affair was that a large number of the German newspapers and magazines, in discussing the matter, made light of it. They actually sought to condone the offence by most shameless arguments. They maintained that the code of morality proper for the crowded cities of Europe was out of place in the wilderness of Africa. They said that it was foolish to punish or even condemn in Germany, acts committed in Africa. They even pleaded ennui and the imperative necessity of amusement as excuses for the German officers. As for the idea that Leist and his men had been criminally cruel, that was absurd, for those whom Leist had abused, were, after all, 'only niggers.' They had simply assisted nature in her work of exterminating a lower species; they had exemplified the law of the survival of the fittest. Such arguments were everywhere read and endorsed.

"Those who most openly objected to the expression of such ideas were not persons who were prominent in the German government. They were not the members of the solid, substantial, conservative parties, but the younger and more radical spirits,

who have taken up with all sorts of socialistic here-
sies and ideas about the 'rights of the people.' It
was they, and not the slow-going, law-abiding citizens, who held indignation meetings at the time the
facts in the Leist case were developing."

Sample Vegetarians.

A native of Maine (France) informs me that in his
grandfather's time the peasants of that department
enjoyed far longer life and more robust health than
the present generation who have exchanged the simple sustenance of former years for a dietary consisting largely of stimulating drinks and animal food.
Examples of this kind are not far to seek and might
be indefinitely multiplied, whether with regard to
races, communities, or families.

If from national generalities we pass to the consideration of individual experience of the Pythagorean system, we are met by such an enormous mass
of evidence as would require volumes to chronicle it.
Let a few instances, chosen from thousands, suffice;
the limits of this little treatise preclude more numerous citations.

The celebrated Lord Heathfield, who defended
the fortress of Gibraltar with consummate skill and
persevering fortitude, was well known for his hardy
habits of military discipline. He neither ate animal
food nor drank wine; his constant diet being bread
and vegetables, and his drink, water.

"My health," says Mr. Jackson, a distinguished
surgeon in the British army, "has been tried in all
ways and climates; and by the aid of temperance

and hard work, I have worn out two campaigns and probably could wear out another. I eat no animal food, drink no wine, malt liquors, nor spirits of any kind. I wear no flannel, and regard neither wind nor rain, heat nor cold."

Professor Lawrence knew a lady who, having adopted a vegetarian mode of life, was remarkable for her activity and strength. She made nothing of walking ten miles, and could with ease walk twenty. She had two children, and nursed them for about twelve months each, during which time she took only vegetables and fruit, with distilled water as drink. Both children were fine and healthy.

Another lady (the wife of one of the founders of the Vegetarian Society in England) abstained from flesh and all intoxicants for thirty years, and during that time, gave birth to fifteen children, fourteen of whom she nursed herself and yet remained young and active.

The celebrated reformer of the eighteenth century, John Wesley, wrote to the Bishop of London in 1747, that, following the advice of Dr. Cheyne, he had given up the use of flesh-meat and wine, and that from that time, thanks to God, he had been delivered from all physical ills.

In the month of October, 1878, a Jewish rabbi named Hirsch Guttman, died at Gross-Strehlitz at the advanced age of 108 years. He had been a vegetarian for half a century. Rabbi Guttman was presented to the Emperor of Germany, who, after a long conversation with the old man, respectfully received his blessing.

The Vegetarian Turk.

I observed, on a late journey to Constantinople, that the boatmen or rowers of the caiques, who are perhaps the best rowers in the world, drink nothing but water; and they drink that profusely during the hot months of the summer.   The boatmen and water-carriers of Constantinople are decidedly, in my opinion, the finest men in Europe, as regards their physical development, and they are all water-drinkers; they may take a little sherbet at times. Their diet is chiefly bread; now and then a cucumber, with cherries, figs, dates, mulberries, or other fruits which are abundant there; now and then a little fish.

From the day of his irruption into Europe the Turk has always proved himself to be endowed with singularly strong vitality and energy.   As a member of a warlike race, he is without equal in Europe in health and hardiness.   He can live and fight when soldiers of any other nationality would starve.   His excellent physique, his simple habits, his abstinence from intoxicating liquors, and his normal vegetarian diet, enable him to support the greatest hardships, and to exist on the scantiest and simplest food.

Low stature is the exception in the Ottoman army. These men of herculean form are endowed with fabulous sobriety; they drink no intoxicating drinks, and seldom touch meat.

Some of the men among the Turkish excavators were remarkably adroit in throwing up the sand, which they would cast up even as high as twelve feet.   Their food was of the simplest kind; coarse bread and a little salt fish or olives, black raisins and some fruit occasionally, accompanied by copious draughts of the best water they could obtain, constituted their breakfast and dinner. To their supper, as being the most sumptuous meal, some delicacy, such as thistle broth, boiled thistle stalks, snail-soup, dandelion, and other wild vegetables, were often added. With this frugal diet their strength was unusually great, as the fatigues which they endured, in spite of the unhealthy climate, and the great weights which they carried in their arms or on their backs, sufficiently proved. The Turkish porters in Smyrna often carry from four hundred to six hundred pounds weight on their backs, and a merchant one day pointed out to me one of his men who, he assured me, had carried an enormous bale of merchandise weighing eight hundred pounds up an incline into an upper warehouse.

In Smyrna, where there are no carts or wheel-carriages, the carrying business falls upon the shoulders of the porters, who are seen in great numbers about the wharves and docks and in the streets near the water-side, where they are employed in lading and unlading vessels. They are stout, robust men, of great muscular strength, and carry at one load, upon a pad fitted to their backs, from four hundred to eight hundred pounds.—*The Perfect Way in Diet.*

Society Reports.

THE VEGETARIAN SOCIETY, NEW YORK.

EXECUTIVE COMMITTEE FOR 1896.

President,   JOHN WALTER SCOTT.
First Vice-President,   MRS. M. A. HAVILAND.
Second Vice-President,   GEORGE BRUNSWICK.
Treasurer,   CHARLES A. MONTGOMERY.
Secretary,   ARTHUR HAVILAND.

Regular Meetings held on the fourth Wednesday in the month at 27 West 42nd street.

53RD REGULAR MEETING.

At the meeting of the Vegetarian Society, New York, held at Fifth Avenue Hall, 27 West 42nd street, September 23, the discussion of the topic "Vegetarianism from a Woman's Standpoint" was quite general and interesting.

Miss Marie G. Luksch, of Vienna, teacher of vocal music, sang Shelley's "Love Song" and the "Magic Song."

A circular of the Vegetarian Federal Union relating the spread of the movement as a part of their work for the Jubilee year, was read.

In the discussion attention was called to the many relations of Vegetarianism to woman's life and work, as she appears as the mistress of servants, the provider of meals, the housekeeper, the cook and the mother.

It was stated that the very large increase in the consumption of cereals was due to the spread of vegetarianism, and that a still greater refinement in our meals would be had by the use of flowers both for

ornament and for food, as nasturtium, violets, arbut-
alon, etc.

Mr. Scott thought that the prevalent carnivorous
habits of the people entailed great hardship on the
gentler sex; familiarizing them with disgusting
sights such as the preparation of dead animals for
cooking, without counting their practical enslavement
by the large portion of their time which was occupied
in marketing, cooking and clearing up after such an
unholy repast. Man was clearly a frugiverous animal and when he returns to his natural diet nine-
tenths of the drudgery of his female partner will be
done away with. There are many vegetarians in
this country, some in the colder portions, whose food
consisted solely of uncooked fruits and nuts, and
while it may not be possible for us all to follow their
cleanly and healthful example, there is not the slightest difficulty for any person living in a civilized country, securing proper nourishment from the vegetable
kingdom without degrading themselves to the level
of the lower orders of animals by killing and devour-
ing the bodies of those weaker than themselves.

Miss Luksch remarked that while the selection of
food and the cooking of it was very important, still
there were many kinds of food which were better
raw—more nutritious—for instance, when served in
the form of salads.

Miss Bedford, teacher of cooking, said that in
summer it was advisable to omit the eating of vegetables, and also that the statement that vegetarian
cooking did not require such hot fires in the kitchen
was ill-advised, as some vegetables need as hot a fire
and for as long a time as meats, and some meats

need but a few minutes of the fire. Meat-eaters eat something besides meat; a properly constituted meal consists of 4 parts of carbon (starch), and 1 part of meat; still we Americans especially do not pay sufficient attention to vegetarianism, which would be more generally practiced if the idea of the preservation of the health could be strengthened. Again, there are parasites attached to vegetables to offset the germs in the meats, of which the vegetarians talk so much.

Mr. Scott remarked that a sudden change of diet was not only possible but proper; no bad effects follow; a person's diet might be unvaried throughout the year, and if properly selected for the system, health and weight remain the same even with great mental labor and without physical exercise. He called attention to the fact that prior to the 16th century the food of the people of Europe was largely meat, and that leprosy and other blood diseases were common; and the scourge was only mitigated by the introduction of the potato from America, which was probably the greatest benefit to Europe accruing from Columbus' voyage.

Mr. Turner said that our health is in the hands of the women and if vegetarianism is best *they* ought to know it. Ordinarily people will not suffer from not eating meat, which is a stimulant the same as alcohol, in this that it contains material which the body cannot use and must throw off promptly, necessitating increased activity of all the digestive, circulatory and excretory apparatus. If all the cells of ox-meat were sound, evidently no better food could be had than meat, but there are three classes of cells in all living flesh—growing, perfect, decaying, and of the three, only one can be used by the human system. If you can convince people that meat is not necessary, you will do a great deal. The mistake of vegetarians is that they decry the steak but provide no substitute.

All conditions are against the possibility of good meat and even that is the poorest food.

His position was strongly combatted by Messrs. Scott and Montgomery, with whom humanity is the first consideration, preceding even that of life.

Mr. C. A. Montgomery called attention to a disgusting and brutal exhibition that was advertised to take place in the outskirts of Brooklyn where oxen were to be killed before a gathering of men, women and children to determine the respective skill of two butchers. After some discussion Miss S. E. Fuller offered the following:

"RESOLVED: that the Vegetarian Society, New York, respectfully appeals to the Mayor of Brooklyn to use whatever power he may have to prevent the *public killing* of oxen in a contest advertised to take place at C. Wissel's Ridgewood Park, Brooklyn, on Thursday, October 1. The Vegetarian Society believes that such an exhibition would be *demoralizing* to the women and children witnessing it, and not in harmony with our advance; *therefore* this Society asks that the slaughter of the animals shall be in an *abattoir* or other private place, without witnesses other than those required to do the killing and preparation of the meat for the barbecue."

Adjourned.

ARTHUR HAVILAND, *Secretary.*

THE VEGETARIAN.

SUBSCRIPTION:

Per Year, prepaid, to any part of the World, ... 25 cents.
10 Subscriptions, to different addresses . . . . . . $1.00.
Single copies, 2 cents; 50 cents per 100.

Published Monthly by
The Vegetarian Publishing Company, 40 John Street, New York City.

Entered at the New York Post Office as Second-class matter.

VOL. II.   NOVEMBER 15, 1896.   NO. 5.

Healthy Living.

BY JOHN SMITH, OF MALTON.

I do not expect that those of my readers who enjoy what they consider good health will be induced to test for themselves the truth of the views advocated in this work. They will perhaps say, "It is all very well for those to adopt a fruit and farinaceous diet who find a necessity for so doing; but, as we possess excellent health, and enjoy our food, we are satisfied that a mixed diet agrees with us best, and, therefore, shall make no change, but 'let well alone.'" They may think that constitutions are different, and that the food which agrees with some may not suit others. To such I would only observe that the digestive and chylo-poietic organs of all men are formed after one type, and that constitutions differ merely by slight congenital peculiarities, modified by long habit; and these differences would prove no serious obstacle to the gradual adoption of a more natural diet. If fruit and farinacea be the natural and best food of man, there cannot be a doubt that all would find this diet more conducive to perfect health, real pleasure and long life, than any other. But let no one attempt the change who is not convinced that great benefits are to be derived from it, or who is not determined to bear patiently the inconveniences that may be at first experienced. To commence requires great self-denial, and to reap all the pleasures and advantages that result, demands great perseverance. Unless, therefore, the mind be firmly resolved, the desire for more tasty and stimulating food will be continually recurring; and, so long as this is the case, no relish will be acquired for more simple fare. I should be sorry to induce any one to make such alterations in his mode of living as would diminish his pleasures or interfere with the real enjoyment of life, and must leave each to adopt that course which he thinks will secure to him the most permanent felicity. "Let every man be fully persuaded in his own mind: prove all things and hold fast that which is good." Many, however, who are suffering from disease, will be disposed to make trial of a diet which promises so many advantages; and it is to such that the following cautions and advice are more particularly addressed.

The generality of persons who have not lived on a full animal diet may at once make the change without experiencing much inconvenience; but others will find it safer to adopt a fruit and farinaceous diet by degrees, and to permit a few weeks to elapse before they live on it exclusively. It has been already stated that the gastric juice and other secretions vary with the character of the food; slight indisposition, therefore, may attend any sudden change of diet. It has also been shown that when a stimulating diet has been exchanged for a simple yet nutritious one, the circulation and respiration will probably become slower; the physical force may appear diminished; the frame may become languid, and the spirits less buoyant. No one, however, need be alarmed at these effects; they are but temporary, and will soon be succeeded by more agreeable sensations. Prejudices against an exclusively vegetable diet are so strong that those who commence it are apt to attribute to its use every disagreeable feeling, and every deviation from health which they experience, regardless of many other circumstances which may have been the real cause. It must not be expected that the trial of a few weeks, or even of a few months, will be sufficient to eradicate any serious disease; some progress may be made in that time, but Nature is slow in all her operations, and it is necessary that the whole of the blood and a considerable portion of the tissues, should be renewed before a complete state of health can be expected. In simpler and less dangerous disorders a state of convalescence is very often produced remarkably soon. Medicine may in many cases succeed in effecting a cure much more rapidly; but, without a proper attention to diet, there is a continual danger of a recurrence. Those who have been in the habit of taking much animal food should commence the change with farinaceous articles, or preparations from them (such as rice, sago, barley, wheaten flour, oatmeal, potatoes, etc.), rather than with fruits, either ripe or preserved; but these will be found very beneficial if gradually introduced. Care should be taken that the bread employed is not made from flour of too fine a quality, as it very frequently produces constipation. Undressed meal is decidedly the most wholesome.

No operations are more necessary to be performed by the vegetable eater than due mastication and insalivation; for, unless these important processes be attended to, indigestion is almost sure to be the consequence. Chymification commences in the stomach on the surface of each individual fragment of food; consequently, the smaller the particles into which it is comminuted by the teeth, the sooner it will be digested. The saliva has a considerable influence on farinaceous food, and the glands which secrete it are large in all herbivorous and frugivorous animals. This fluid is alkaline, and it is worthy of remark that when any of the alkalies are taken for the purpose of neutralizing morbid acidity of the stomach, the nature of the saliva is entirely changed, and it assumes quite an opposite property. Many, therefore, produce serious mischief by neglecting to employ an antidote supplied by nature, while they officiously substitute artificial preparations. Acidity, heartburn, etc., would frequently be easily removed if the patient would voluntarily excite an increased flow of saliva, and continue to swallow it for a few minutes; but this would seldom be necessary if proper food were used and carefully masticated.

Each meal should be carefully digested before another is taken, and a period of repose should always succeed a period of activity. When the sensation of

hunger is experienced in less time than six hours
after each meal, it may be generally considered as a
morbid craving, dependent on imperfect chylifica-
tion, in consequence of the too frequent ingestion
of food interrupting the ventricular and cœcal digestion. The faintness usually experienced by the
dyspeptic is only increased by frequent eating and is
most readily removed by fasting.

Moderate exercise in the open air, for the purpose
of assisting the various secretions, is another essential requisite for the production and maintenance of
good health. None can long neglect this rule with
impunity; but a sedentary life is certainly not so
detrimental to those who live on vegetable food, as
to those who live on an animal or mixed diet. Unless
sufficient oxygen be supplied to the lungs by daily
exercise in the open air, the products of decomposition fail to be removed in sufficient quantity for the
maintenance of a healthy state, and the assimilation
of new matter is impeded. Without exercise, also,
"the contractile power of the heart and large arteries
is feebly exerted; and, though sufficient to carry the
blood to the ultimate tissue, it is nevertheless not
strong enough to carry it through with rapidity necessary for health. The ultimate tissue being thus filled
faster than it is emptied, congestion takes place in
those delicate and important vessels which compose
it, as well as in the large veins, the office of which
is to convey the blood from this tissue to the heart.
One of the chief conditions of the body, in that general ill state of health usually denominated 'indigestion,' is congestion of blood in the ultimate tissue of
our organs—the brain, the lungs, the spinal marrow,

the stomach, the ganglionic system, the liver, bowels, and all the organs concerned in the nutrition of the body." When the system, therefore, undebilitated by disease, will admit a good supply of oxygen by muscular exercise, it is the best means of diminishing the amount of venous blood, and (in conjunction with a legitimate supply of proper food) of increasing the amount of arterial blood; and, in proportion as the latter preponderates over the former, shall we possess health and muscular strength, as well as elasticity of mind.

"Oxygen," says Mr. E. Johnson, "is the only stimulating drink which we can.take with advantage to ourselves, for the purpose of invigorating our strength and elevating our animal spirits. It is the wine and spirit of life—the true *eau de vie*, with an abundance of which nature has supplied us ready made, and it is the only one proper to man. If you be thristy, drink water; if low-spirited, drink oxygen; that is to say, take active exercise, during which you inhale it." Violent exercise, however, should be avoided; for, though consistent with health, it renders the processes of decay and renewal too rapid, and hastens the period of old age.

The skin, being a very important excretory organ, should on no consideration be neglected. About thirty ounces of the worn-out materials of the body are said to escape (by insensible perspiration) in twenty-four hours; but the quantity varies with the temperature of the atmosphere, the amount of exercise, and other circumstances. The innumerable pores by which effete matter abounding in carbon and nitrogen are excreted, can perform their function with much greater freedom in the herbivora than in man; because the artificial clothing which the latter is under the necessity of using in cold climates prevents free exhalation and the skin becomes sheathed in an oleaginous compound, which materially checks the necessary process. The consequence is that the lungs, kidneys and liver have additional duty to discharge, which frequently terminates in functional or organic disease. Hence arises the necessity for frequent ablution, in order to preserve the normal condition of the perspiratory pores. The warm bath, or sponging the whole surface of the body with tepid water, will effectually remove all extraneous matter from the skin; but, as warmth is debilitating and cold (when judiciously administered) is a powerful tonic, it is desirable that cold water should be substituted whenever the constitution will permit it. Many who have been extremely liable to coughs, sore throats, etc., have by this means been completely protected against a recurrence of these distressing and dangerous complaints. Nearly all who are not affected with organic disease may bear the cold bath, or cold sponging, in all seasons, with considerable advantage to health; but its daily use will prove injurious if the body be exposed too long to the influence of cold, and, unless a reaction and moisture of the surface be promoted by subsequent muscular exercise, or by friction of the skin with the hand, the hair glove or the flesh brush.

Several other rules for the preservation of health may be here mentioned, such as regular hours, early rising, good ventilation of the sitting and sleeping rooms, avoidance of currents of air, and some others, the importance of which is so generally acknowledged that they require no recommendation.—*Fruits and Farinacea*.

The Thanksgiving Banquet.

We copy from the *Chicago Vegetarian* the following particulars of an interesting banquet which will be given by the Chicago Society on Thanksgiving Day. We trust that many Eastern vegetarians will be able to join their ·Western brethren on that day and enjoy the good things which have been prepared to regale their friends and to tempt the cannibals from their depraved tastes:

The festival hall of the Auditorium Hotel will be the scene of a fleshless feast on November 26— Thanksgiving Day. At that time and place the Chicago Vegetarian Society will hold its second annual holiday banquet.

A large attendance is anticipated, and the success of the affair is already assured.

The food question will be discussed from various points of view—the physiological, the hygienic, the ethical, the economic, the religious.

The list of speakers includes the names of a number of well-known reformers.

Rev. H. S. Clubb, of Philadelphia, President of the National Society of Vegetarians, will respond to the toast of "The Vegetarian Society of America."

Miss Frances E. Willard, Virchand R. Grandhi, the Hindoo philosopher; George Francis Train, Annie Jennes-Miller, President John W. Scott, of the New York Vegetarian Society; Dr. J. H. Kellogg, Sir Alexander Ross, President of the Food Reform Society of Canada; Governor Altgeld, and others equally prominent, have been invited to talk.

H. S. Wilcox, Recording Secretary of the Society, will act as toastmaster, and will doubtless fill the position with judgment and good taste. Mr. Wilcox is a well-known lawyer and an ex-newspaper man.

The bill of fare will be all that can be desired—even by Vegetarians—and variety will not be lacking.

Perhaps the chief feature of this menu of many features will be the "vegetable roast," which will be made from " Nuttose," a nut preparation which, when cooked, is so perfect a substitute for roast beef that in eating it one could readily imagine himself partaking of flesh food. This vegetable roast contains exactly the same proportion of proteids, or nitrogenous matter, as beefsteak, and, in addition, thirty per cent. of fat, and a rich supply of the nerve-building and bone-building salts. Besides it is far more digestible and more delicate and toothsome in flavor.

The following has been prepared as a basis of the menu for the banquet by a committee consisting of Mesdames Corinne Brown, J. Bell Bombough, Anna Weeks, and Viola Ludden, M. D., and F. G. Wilhelm:

THE MENU.

Canopeis a la Dusenberry
Cream of Celery a la Clubb
Olives Radishes Celery
Petite Boacheis a la Voltaire
Potatoes a la Parisienne

Croquettes de Rice a la Plato
French Peas
Timbal of Macaroni a la Aristotle
Haricot vert
Vegetarian Roast a la Kellogg
Salad a la Shelley
Dessert

Cream a la Rousseau   Nesselrode Pudding
Fruits   Nuts   Raisins
Almond Meal   Granose
Cereal Coffee   Sterilized Water

Every care has been taken to provide for the pleasant entertainment of those who attend. The guests will be received in the parlors at seven o'clock. The Reception Committee will see to it that everybody becomes acquainted with everybody else. Music is to be provided, and everything will be done to make the occasion an enjoyable one.

The Auditorium is one of the most beautiful hotels in the world, and is known far and wide for the excellence of its banquets. In all its features, including its furnishings and fittings in every department, the Auditorium is without its superior anywhere in the world.

While the banquet will be given by the Vegetarian Society, and in the interests of vegetarianism, it is not the intention to confine the sale of tickets to vegetarians only. Every person interested in the betterment of mankind and who takes pleasure in meeting those who entertain like sentiments, is especially invited to participate in the enjoyment that the festive convocation at the Auditorium will offer. Those residing outside of Chicago who desire to attend are requested to write to the treasurer for information regarding hotels, transportation, etc.

Orders for tickets should be sent in as soon as possible. They should be addressed to Miss Frances L. Dusenberry, Treasurer Chicago Vegetarian Society, McVicker's Building, Chicago.

The cost of the ticket is $2.00.

The Society has been officially informed that the railroad companies will sell railroad tickets for Thanksgiving Day at either half fare or a fare and one-third for the round trip.

Clippings.

VEGETARIANS FROM NECESSITY.—Speaking at a dinner given by the Merchant Tailors' Company, on the 20th of May (the *Guardian*, 27th May, 1885, p. 798, col. 1), Bishop Temple said: "He could hardly speak too strongly on the subject of the distress which had fallen upon the clergy. . . . He had known a clergyman who had had to live for months entirely upon vegetables; he had known a benefice whose normal value was £600 a year, from which the incumbent could not get £60; he had known a clergyman who for three or four weeks together had been unable to get anything to eat but bread."

STUFFED EGGS.—Boil six eggs for twenty minutes. Remove the shells and cut lengthwise. Mash the yolks, add one teaspoonful of butter, a little chopped parsley, thyme, or other herbs as preferred, salt and pepper. Fill the whites with the mixture; press the two halves together. Put them into a baking dish and cover with white sauce made of one tablespoonful of butter, one tablespoonful of flour, and one cup of hot milk. Season with salt and pepper; then cover with buttered crumbs, and brown.

OBERLIN'S KITCHEN.—"What is this iron pan suspended over your lamp on the table? "That is my kitchen," said Oberlin; "I dine with my parents, who allow me to bring away with me each time a lump of bread. At eight o'clock in the evening I put the bread in this pan, with a little salt. I pour some water on it, then I put my lamp under it, and continue my studies. If toward ten or eleven o'clock I feel hungry, I then eat the soup which I have made in this way, and I can tell you I find it very delicious food." The Oberlin family were nurtured upon fare which does not sustain some of the modern theories of what is essential for the strengthening of the human frame. The *menu* from year to year was much as follows:. "Potatoes and milk. Brown bread and milk. Potatoes and green vegetables pleasantly cooked with milk. Rice boiled in milk, eaten with oatcake. Fruit with bread, corn flour made into a pudding with milk."—*Life of Oberlin*, by Mrs. Josephine Butler.

EXTRACTS FROM BACKHOUSE AND TYLOR'S "WITNESS FOR CHRIST," VOL. I.—One meal only a day was allowed (to Basil's monks) of bread, water and beans, without salt. "With us," wrote Basil to the Emperor Julian, "as is becoming, the cook's art has no place; our knives never touch blood; our daintiest meal is vegetables, with coarse bread, and half sour wine" (p. 55). By the labor of Basil's monks many a barren tract was converted into corn-fields and vineyards (p. 54). "Send me some fine potherbs," wrote Gregory Nazienzen to a friend who, with Basil, was about to pay him a visit, "if thou dost not wish to see Basil hungry and cross" (p. 53, note).

George Bernard Shaw, the London novelist, who has been a vegetarian for fifteen years, says that "the enormity of eating the scorched corpses of animals—cannibalism with its heroic dish omitted—becomes impossible the moment it becomes consciously instead of thoughtlessly habitual."

RUSSIAN ARMY RATIONS.—Where an Englishman would be half starved, the Russian finds his ration sufficient. According to the "Armed Strength of Russia," the men receive a mess allowance which is calculated to give them one-third of a pound of meat on 199 days of the year. The remaining 169 days are observed as fasts according to the rules of the Greek Church! In addition, about two pounds of flour, which the men bake into bread for themselves, or 1lb. 13 oz. of biscuits, is issued per man, and to this is added 4 4-5 ounces of groats, 4-5 ounce of salt, and for every 100 men 117-10 ounces of tea, and 2lbs. 3 3-10 ounces of sugar. As against this, the daily feed ration of the British soldier is 1lb. of meat, 1 1-2lb. of bread or 1lb. biscuit, 1-3 oz. coffee, 1-6 oz. tea, 2 oz. sugar, and 1-2 oz. salt, and when hard work is being done another 1-2lb. of meat is added, if possible, and it is also usual to serve out 2 oz. compressed vegetables, or 4 oz. preserved potatoes. At home groceries and vegetables are not issued as rations, but a sum not exceeding 3d. a day is stopped out of the men's pay to form a mess fund,

out of which they supply themselves with such ex-
tras.—*Blackwood's Magazine.*

The *Malvern Looker-on* has the following paragraph on Vegetarian Restaurants. "You must
know that I have a friend, a fat little man and as
happy as any mortal living, and one day he gave a
severe shock to all my preconceived notions of
things by telling me he was a Vegetarian. It was a
self-evident fact that he was not half-starved, and
after thinking over the problem for some time, I
made up my mind to pay a visit to a Vegetarian
Restaurant, and solve the mystery. Well, having
carried this resolve into effect, and finding myself
seated in a nice, bright, cheery apartment, waited
on by a comely little maid in tidy habiliments, I
took up the bill of fare. I could make nothing of
the uncouth names before me—they were as in-
scrutable as the Sphinx—and finally, with a wild
guess, I gave an order, choosing the easiest word I
could find. What the particular order was does not
matter. Suffice it to say, the most exacting epicure
could hardly have found fault with the dish I was
served with, It was some sort of pie, the contents
being very eatable, but what they consisted of I
would rather not say ; the crust was the most delicate and ethereal ever put together by mortal fingers
—a veritable fairy confection ; nicer, more palatable
dishes I have seldom met, while the cooking was
simply perfection. If any of my lady-readers should
happen to visit the metropolis they cannot do better
than pay a visit to a Vegetarian Restaurant; they
will find the *menu* a delightful change from the con-
ventional dishes of most modern dining-rooms."

Society Reports.

THE VEGETARIAN SOCIETY, NEW YORK.

EXECUTIVE COMMITTEE FOR 1896.

President, JOHN WALTER SCOTT.
First Vice-President, MRS. M. A. HAVILAND.
Second Vice-President, GEORGE BRUNSWICK.
Treasurer, CHARLES A. MONTGOMERY.
Secretary, ARTHUR HAVILAND.

Regular Meetings held on the fourth Wednesday in the month at 27 West 42nd street.

54TH REGULAR MEETING.

At the meeting of the Vegetarian Society, New York, held at the Fifth Avenue Hall, on October 28th, Vice President Brunswick presiding and 28 members and visitors present, Mr. C. A. Montgomery opened the discussion on the Topic, " Apples from Adam to date," by stating the history of the fruit, and the estimation of its many good qualities held by ancient and modern writers, in the poetic, scientific and practical realms. The discussion was well maintained by many persons, all of whom united in praise of its usefulness as food, in both health and sickness.

The next meeting will be held on the 23d inst. at same place, at which President H. S. Clubb of the general Vegetarian Society will attend and the Topic will be " What is the best food".

The Vegetarian.

Volume I., attractively bound in linen, 236 pages, price $1.00

Contains many valuable articles on the subject and would make a suitable present for Vegetarians or thinking people.

THE PERFECT WAY IN DIET.

A treatise advocating a return to the natural and ancient food of our race.

—BY—

ANNA KINGSFORD,

Doctor of Medicine of the Faculty of Paris,

Sixth Edition, 1895. Price $1.00, Post Free.

THE VEGETARIAN PUBLISHING CO., 40 John St., New York.

THE VEGETARIAN·

SUBSCRIPTION:

Per Year, prepaid, to any part of the World, ... 25 cents.
10 Subscriptions, to different addresses . . . . . $1.00.
Single copies, 2 cents; 50 cents per 100.

Published Monthly by
The Vegetarian Publishing Company, 40 John Street, New York City.

Entered at the New York Post Office as Second-class matter.

VOL. II.   DECEMBER 15, 1896.   No. 6.

Chauncey Roe.

There are vegetarians and vegetarians; the name is the same in both cases but the spirit is different; would that there were more like the man whose name is given above. It is very easy to give up eating flesh, and probably there are cases where the individual is not improved thereby, but the motive is of far greater importance than the action. I certainly would be the last to censure a savage for being a cannibal, or of the ignorant masses in our large cities for eating flesh. Mr. Roe has been a vegetarian for several years and was converted by reading a paper by Lady Wall-Paget, published in the "*Nineteenth Century*." In gratitude for the benefits received he has had the article reprinted, and is distributing it broadcast in the hopes that others may be turned from the error of their ways, even as he was. If every convert would follow his example the world would be the better for it and the spread of truth be accelerated.

Perhaps the strongest paragraph in the pamphlet is the following;

"I do not think that anybody has the right to indulge in tastes which oblige others to follow a brutalizing occupation, which morally degrades the man who earns his bread by it. To call a man a butcher means that he is fond of bloodshed. Butchers often become murderers. I remember two cases in the papers last summer where butchers had been hired to murder individuals whom they did not even know. After this comes the irrepressible thought, Is it right to take life in order to feed one's self, when there is plenty of other available food which will do just as well? * * * A more serious consideration, and one which grew upon me every year, was the sad and distasteful necessity of killing a living being in order to live one's self. The great mystery of pain in this world, which if it once gets a hold upon the mind is so terribly difficult to shake off, often dimmed my greatest pleasures. But this feeling too I tried, but less successfully, to subordinate to what I then considered right and reasonable."

The Chicago Banquet.

The December number of the *Chicago Vegetarian* brings the best account we have so far received of the Thanksgiving day banquet held in that city. It was a great and deserved success. The thanks of humanity are due its originators and those who, by their presence, helped to shed lustre on the occasion.

Among the speakers were our old friend Henry S. Clubb, President of the Vegetarian Society of America, Albert H. Snyder, President of the Chicago Vegetarian Society, Mrs. Fairchild Allen of the Illinois Anti-Vivisection Society, Anagarika H. Dharmapala and many others. Music and singing was provided by the Misses Mabelle Lewis, Adele Blauer, Daisy Bombaugh, Alice Bateman and Jennie Woody.

The toast of the evening was given by Mr. Clubb and is reproduced below.

" The sentiment given in such a kind and complimentary spirit, and so cordially received by you, is another evidence, added to many others, of the hearty and generous feelings which have ever existed between the Chicago Vegetarian Society and the one which I have the honor to represent and which covers in its aspiration this vast continent of America. Although in its infancy, it already operates in all the United States and Territories, in the British possessions and also to some extent in Mexico and other Southern republics.

" There certainly has never been any reason why this cordiality should not exist and why this hearty co-operation should not continually increase. It was the Vegetarian Society of America that selected Chicago for the holding of the Whole World's Vegetarian Congress in 1893—a Congress that has done so much to place the humane and merciful sentiments of vegetarian advocates before the world. These results were secured by the united efforts of the Chicago society and the Vegetarian Society of America for at least two years previous to that event. Although so much was accomplished by the active co-operation of these societies and the representatives of the Vegetarian Federal Union, and of the Vegetarian Society of Manchester, England, it is a fact that the principal truths presented and discussions held have only been briefly presented to the public. What would have been accomplished had the full report appeared can be only conjectured. That report is still in our hands and the Vegetarian Society of America having now a press of its own, is preparing to issue a volume containing all that valuable material and hopes with the co-operation of Chicago, New York and other large cities, and of the vegetarians scattered throughout the continent, to place this compilation in all the public libraries of the world, so as to justify the title of the "Whole World's Vegetarian Congress."

"Attending this beautiful banquet, which is held to set an example to mankind of blending the principles of humanity and kindness with our Thanksgiving festival, to show that the sacrifice of life is not necessary to our gratitude or enjoyment, reminds me of a similar reform introduced about 1860 years ago.

"It had been customary from a traditional practice of the House of Israel to make an annual feast, called the Passover, and at this feast an innocent lamb was the victim and its slaughtered remains were partaken of by the guests. (Now the yearly victim is an innocent, harmless bird, called a turkey). But then there came a great Innovator who had a little company of apostles. And he taught them the best way of showing their gratitude to their Heavenly Father for rescuing them from Egyptian bondage and the bondage of sin. It is said He took not a leg of the calf, but a loaf of bread, gave thanks and broke it, and gave to the disciples and said: "Take, eat; this is my body which is given for you; this do in remembrance of me." And he took the cup in like manner and gave thanks, and gave to them, saying: "This cup is the new covenant in my blood which is poured out for you. Drink ye all of this. This do as oft as ye drink in remembrance of me." And they all drank of it. This was the first vegetarian banquet under the new dispensation, and it has been adopted in nearly all Christian churches and has superseded the animal sacrifice.

"It is true the institutor of this new and merciful order of worship was, so far as his material body was concerned, made a victim, but he rose again from the dead and his birth and resurrection are celebrated at two of the great festivals, called Christmas and Easter, and all men are being drawn unto him.

"We are also reminded by this banquet of one which we attended in the city of Manchester, England, July 28, 1848, forty-eight years ago. It was held, as this is, at one of the hotels of the city. It had a bill of fare consisting of two courses:

"First course.—Large Savory Omelet with Vegetables. Rice Fritters with Vegetables and Beet-Root. Sage and Onion Fritters with Vegetables. Savory Pie. Mushroom Pie with Vegetables. Bread and Parsley Fritters. Forcemeat. Fritters with Vegetables. Macaroni Omelet. Water the only beverage.

"Second Course.—Flummery. Gooseberries, Creams. Nuts. Cheesecakes. Red and White

Currants. Moulded Sago. Fruit Tarts. Water. Sponge Cake, etc.

"The tables were appropriately decorated with vases of flowers. In the minister's blessing occurred these words: "We come to Thee with the more confidence on this occasion, inasmuch that we are sure that this is—and we thankfully acknowledge it—a guiltless feast upon which we may hopefully invoke thy benediction." This banquet was presided over by Joseph Brotherton, a member of the British parliament who had then followed the vegetarian practice about forty years.

"Since that time many vegetarian banquets have been held in various parts of England, on the continent of Europe and in New York, Philadelphia and Chicago in America, at some of which it has been my privilege to be present. And what is still more important, the idea of a guiltless feast in the preparation of which no blood has been spilt is being adopted by many families of all civilized nations, and is being extended to thousands of homes that have become blessed with the benign influence which has conferred health and happiness where before was sickness, misery and contention.

"None but those who have experienced it can fully understand the true enjoyment of a home that is free from the stain and odor of flesh and blood. To young persons just beginning domestic life together in the most delightful relationship, we always recommend a *new* house and home where the deathly, sickening odor of slaughtered flesh has never entered.

"Pure homes are essential to pure lives. It is much easier to begin right than to get right after beginning with the old pollution and permitting it to contaminate the atmosphere and destroy the sweetness of home.

"Thanking you on behalf of the Vegetarian Society of America for the kindly and complimentary sentiment you have expressed in its honor, permit me to offer as a volunteer sentiment:

"The New Homes of Chicago: may they begin and be continued in the line of purity, humanity, peace and progress, for 'Better is a dinner of herbs where love is than a stalled ox and contention therewith.'"

Society Reports.

THE VEGETARIAN SOCIETY, NEW YORK.

EXECUTIVE COMMITTEE FOR 1896.

President, JOHN WALTER SCOTT.
First Vice-President, MRS. M. A. HAVILAND.
Second Vice-President, GEORGE BRUNSWICK.
Treasurer, CHARLES A. MONTGOMERY.
Secretary, ARTHUR HAVILAND.

Regular Meetings held on the fourth Wednesday in the month at 27 West 42nd street.

55TH REGULAR MEETING.

At the 55th meeting of the Vegetarian Society, New York, held Nov. 23, 1896, at the hall of Fowler & Wells, 27 East 21st street, President Scott in the chair and forty members and visitors present, the Rev. H. S. Clubb, of Philadelphia, President of the American Vegetarian Society, was introduced to speak upon the topic of the evening "What is the best food for man?" He said, that, having lately been occupied with the history of the movement for food reform in America, there were several matters in that discussion which could serve to illustrate the evening's topic, for, its history would tend to show the advantages of vegetarianism. Christ, the profoundest teacher of morality, taught vegetarianism and introduced into the church the sacrament of bread and wine (grape juice), instead of the passover of the Jews which required the slaughter of a lamb. The Christian religion is closely identified with our vegetarian practices, and the early churches were probably vegetarian communities. Other teachers of morality, founders of other religions, were also vegetarians: Zoroaster, Confucius, Pythagoras. In America, in the early part of the eighteenth century, Benjamin Franklin was converted to simple diet by reading Thomas Trejoris' *Way to Health, Long Life and Happiness*, published in 1692. In 1720, in Boston, occurred the first recorded vegetarian practice, when Franklin lived on one dollar per week and often saved half of that, resulting, as he said, in increased "clearness of perception."

Mr. Clubb stated he had been a vegetarian for 58 years, that is, 8 or 10 years prior to the institution of the English Vegetarian Society. In 1848, the opening of the vegetarian crusade was a banquet at Heywood's Hall, Manchester, England, at which Mr. Brotherton, M. P., presided, who stated that he had been a vegetarian for 40 years.

"My wealth does not consist so much in the multitude of my possessions as in the fewness of my wants."

He stated, that his experience and observation

clearly proved that those who refrained from animal food have been preserved in youthful appearance, health and beauty, much beyond the time of those who use animal food.

What of the future? It will be just what we make it by united and decided effort; by working together and putting forth our strength to accomplish best results. The movement is favored by having many men who are willing to work in this cause. In Chicago, Mr. Snyder the president, a young man connected with the press, has organized four societies, besides the Vegetarian Eating Club connected with the University. On Thursday next they will have a Thanksgiving Dinner. In the morning there will be a thanksgiving service tending towards the formation of a church on vegetarian principles, with the keynote of " Love one another."

If we refrain from taking life; if we remain in harmony with the principles not to live by the destruction of the life of other animals, the result must be a better nature. Contrast the characters of carnivorous and graminivorous animals. We say if you will get the best out of life; if you wish to live to enjoy the *best*, you must live upon those simple parts of nature which will tend to nurture a character of the highest moral nature.

Being asked as to his diet, Mr. Clubb replied he used cornmeal, nuts, cocoa, butter, hygienic coffee; had dinner at 6 P. M., consisting of potatoes and three or four other vegetables, nuts, eggs, etc., and used sometimes unfermented grape juice or other fruit juices.

President Scott stated that, in his opinion, fruits

and nuts formed the best food. The desire to eat flesh was inherited not natural. Many persons would like to be vegetarians but feared to make a change in their food; but they should remember that three-fourths of the inhabitants of the earth are vegetarians. As to his habits of eating he said they never varied. He took breakfast at 7.45 A. M., consisting (at this season) of two or three bunches of grapes, oatmeal with cream, half a roll and a cup of coffee. Dinner was at 6 P. M. and consisted of two boiled eggs, a cup of coffee and a roll, sometimes Graham bread. Animals in a state of nature never varied their diet, and the further they went from nature the nearer they approached to sickness.

Dr. M. L. Holbrook said that for those who do not wish to depend upon animal material for food, the best food is: first, grains, of which wheat is the best being a perfect food, then oats, while rice is a more unbalanced diet. Labor and exposure had been maintained without liquor on a western railroad by the distribution of one pound of oatmeal per man per day with other foods. Fatty food was necessarily added to white wheat bread, as oils or butter. The German sour-bread was a balanced diet: Second, fruits, of which the best is grapes, the seeds and skins of which should be rejected.

Different people have different requirements, sedentary persons require their food to be more carefully prepared than the laborer.

Vegetarian diet would be the better, but we can't all come to it.

Fruits and potatoes should not be eaten together as they are not compatible.

Dr. E. G. Day said that vegetarianism was founded upon reasons of ethics, hygiene and economy. We have *no* right to take a life which we did not give. Life is some portion of the Deity running through every gradation up to our plane.

Eighty per cent. of our ills originate in the stomach. As to practical experience, he stated that his diet had been one of utmost simplicity for five or six years, principally fruits and nuts. It is well to eliminate a craving for variety, which is palatal indulgence. The menu in his family did not vary, consisting generally of uncooked vegetables, celery, salads, etc., or baked potatoes sometimes; nuts, every variety of fruits, apples preferred; dates and figs. He had often walked fifteen miles upon a midday meal of nuts, raisins or a piece of chocolate.

Animal tissue is not fit food for man.

Mr. Montgomery said that the best food was that which cost the least labor, and caused the least injury to others.

Mr. Holbrook stated that thirty years ago one of Dr. Trall's patients grew thin on a diet of wheat; he therefore ate peanuts, a quart a day. gained twenty pounds in a month and grew fat. A perfect diet would be softened wheat, fruits and nuts.

Mr. H. Allen Spencer stated that he believed the *best food* to be uncooked grains, fruits and nuts, these with cleanliness, fresh air, exercise and sleep, should make a perfect man.

Thanks of the Society are extended to Mr. Clubb for his visit and inspiriting talk, and he was requested to carry to the Chicago Vegetarian Societies our heartiest greetings and well-wishes.

Adjourned.   A. HAVILAND, *Secretary.*

PHILADELPHIA VEGETARIAN SOCIETY.

President,   A. T. de LEARSY.
Vice President,   MRS. SARAH HEALL.
Treasurer,   WILLIAM BROWN.
Secretary,   MISS E. I. BETTES.

COMMITTEE ON TOPICS.
REV. H. S. CLUBB.   MISS E. I. BETTES.

Monthly meetings are held every third Monday in each month at 8 P.M., in the Lecture Room of the Bible Christian Church, Park avenue, above Montgomery avenue.

19TH REGULAR MEETING.

At the November meeting of the Philadelphia Vegetarian Society an address was delivered, the subject of which was " The Alleged Divine Permission to Eat Every Moving Thing," from the words of Gen. IX. ; 3, 4, 5, namely:

" 3. Every moving thing that liveth shall be meat for you.

4. But *flesh*, with the *life* thereof, the *blood* thereof, shall ye not eat !

5. And surely

(1) Your blood of your lives will I require,
(2) At the hand of every beast will I require it;
(3) And at the hand of man,
(4) And at the hand of every man's brother will I require the life of man."

Owing to the Christmas holidays the next meeting is to be held on the first Monday in January (4th), 1897, at the usual time and place.

The following is a summary of the important address.

It was shown according to the *original* reading of the extract, that the words "moving thing" were a translation of but one Hebrew word *romess*, rendered in the best Lexicon and Young's Concordance "creeper" or, more scientifically, "reptile." Hence, *not every kind* of animal, but *only reptiles* were granted for food to such as desired something more than the vegetable kingdom. To the reader of the English version this translation could not but mislead.

Here lay the first difficulty. The "thing" eaten, it was also noticed had to be "*alive*," or "that liveth" according to v. 3. If alive, it must not be dead, for if dead there was but one place in which to deposit it, namely, not the mouth but the earth where all carcases are placed. Then again, inasmuch as an animal—no matter even when a reptile—could or would not be eaten alive by any but wild beasts, what should the meat-eaters do with this doctrine? Some in the audience suggested that under the circumstances the word "creeper" employed here, could not refer to an *animal*, which could not be eaten *alive* by man, but rather to a *vegetable*, a creeping *plant*. This was urged upon the authority of the late learned Rev. Coward, a good Hebraist. This interpretation seemed no less logical than acceptable, particularly so because, whereas, in v. 3 the *live thing* was allowed to be eaten, in v. 4 "flesh with the life thereof," *i. e.*, flesh still quivering with *life* was *prohibited*. And rather than introduce an idea of contradiction here, the speaker thought this explanation out of the dilemma for meat-eaters the best one. Practically the latter would cease to be meat-eaters.

Here lay the second difficulty which, like the first, had no existence whatever for vegetarians.

The words printed in *italics* in verse 4 were, it was pointed out, unauthorized as well as unnecessary, and obscured the meaning contained therein. If translated according to the original, the author here prohibits three things; (1) flesh, *i. e.* meat, (2) alive, (3) blood.

The 5th verse was shown in its third clause to be *defective* and a moral difficulty was pointed out to exist therein in the path of meat-eaters.

In the first clause—first ten words—God makes every man responsible for the human blood he sheds.

The last clause—last fifteen words—of this (5th verse) clearly teaches that every man is responsible for every other man's life he has taken. In the second clause the Creator employs the following language; "At the hand of every *beast* will I require it," *i. e.*, the life of man the beast takes. Manifestly *the beasts* are here declared *responsible* for the human *life* they take. Now, if the *beast* was rendered *responsible* for the human life it took, the speaker, appealing to the intelligence of the audience, their sense of justice, reason and logic, asked whether the conclusion was not inevitable: that the *person* who takes the life of the beast was equally *responsible for the life of the animal* he takes?

The third clause reads as follows: "And at the hand of man." This line is in so far *defective* as it contains *neither object or predicate*. If it stood isolated it would yield no sense whatever, but from the context we can supply the missing link. The verb in each of the other three clauses is clearly seen to be

"require." In clause two *man* is the *object* of the
subject, namely, *beast*; wherein the beast is made
responsible for the *human* life it takes. In this
clause the beast must necessarily be the *object* for the
taking of whose life God makes *man* the responsible
subject. Supplying, therefore, the missing words
from the context, the third clause given in full reads
as follows, placing the supplied words in *italics;*
"And at the hand of man *will I require the life of
the animal he takes*." This may sound an awful ver-
dict to the ears of meat-eaters. Let them become
vegetarians and at once their conscience become re-
lieved of its heavy burden. The free choice lies
before them.

Recapitulated Gen. 9: 3, 4, 5 would present these
three thoughts:

1. A linguistic and physiological trouble are seen
in v. 3 for meat-eaters, namely, that man may eat
only "creepers"—animal or vegetable, which (?)—
and they must be eaten *alive!*

2. *Flesh* as well as *blood*, and either still quivering with *life*, is *prohibited* in v. 4, which command
forms a very serious physical obstacle in the way of
meat-eating.

3. Man, in v. 5, is made *responsible for the animal life* he takes. Here lies a great *moral trouble.*
God will require at the hand of man the life of the
animal he takes or causes to be taken. And the
evil, it would seem, is more aggravated if the poor
animal is slain in order to eat it, which, as is well
known to the youngest vegetarian, is absolutely
necessary. Indeed, the better way, as every vegetarian can testify, is: "Thou shalt not kill!"

THE
VEGETARIAN·

SUBSCRIPTION:

Per Year, prepaid, to any part of the World, ... 25 cents.
10 Subscriptions, to different addresses . . . . . $1.00.
Single copies, 2 cents; 50 cents per 100.

Published Monthly by
The Vegetarian Publishing Company, 40 John Street, New York City.

Entered at the New York Post Office as Second-class matter.

VOL. II. JANUARY 15, 1897. No. 7.

Diseases of Animals communicated to Man.

The question as to what diseases are communicable
to man from diseased animals used as food is at
present occupying the attention of physicians and
physiologists in this country and on the Continent;
and a variety of experiments are being carried out
with a view to the solution of the numerous problems
involved in this enquiry. A variety of causes has
led to the necessity of arriving at a definite conclusion upon the subject with as little delay as is compatible with the difficulty and importance of the
investigation—among which may be enumerated the
increasing importation of foreign cattle, the extension
of the system of sewage irrigation of land, the general
acceptation of the germ theory of the causation of
epidemics, the certainty of the spread of typhoid and
scarlet fevers by an improper milk supply, and an
attempt to solve the problem of the relatively small

death-rate of the Jewish, as compared with the general, population of Great Britain. Papers were read and a discussion held on the subject at the annual meeting of the British Medical Association at Cambridge during this summer, in the section of Public Health under the presidency of Dr. Acland, the Regius Professor of medicine in the university of Oxford, and the following resolution was agreed to: " That, in the opinion of this section, the subject of the communicability of disease to man by animals used by him as food urgently demands careful enquiry, both in regard to the actual state of our knowledge thereon, and to the legislation which is desirable in connection therewith; and that the Committee of Council of the Association be invited to appoint a Committee for the purpose of reporting on this matter."

From the care taken to provide the Jewish community with animal food free from communicable disease, the question has especial interest for them, and the following summary may be taken as conveying the present consensus of scientific opinion upon the subject.

No doubt can of course arise as to the communicability of the class of diseases in infected cattle known as " parasitic," of which trichinosis may be taken as a type. In these cases the parasite is simply transferred from the flesh of the beast to that of the man, in which it finds a congenial home, and, in the process of its development, frequently produces fatal results. Trichinosis, until recently unknown in this country, is frequently met with in Germany, owing to the custom there of eating pork, particularly in the form of sausages, more than half raw. Thus in Berlin, where the inspection of meat is obligatory, fifteen outbreaks of the malady were officially reported during the year 1878; and in one of the suburban districts, half of those affected died. The immunity of Great Britain from trichinosis is unfortunately a thing of the past, two outbreaks having been recognised during the past decade—one in Wokington in 1871, and a second on board the schoolship "Cornwall" in 1877, both traceable to the use of pork as food, in one case home-fed, in the second imported from America. The case against meat infected with parasites, of which there are several distinct varieties, is so clearly proved that no object can be gained by discussing it further.

With this exception, the animal diseases which are at present, or have been, regarded as transmissible to man through ingested meat are seven in number, viz, (1) cattle-plague, (2) swine-typhoid, (3) pleuropneumonia, (4) foot-and-mouth disease, (5) anthracoid diseases, (6) erysipelas, and (7) tubercle. As regards the first two, the evidence as to their power of specific infection when taken as food is conflicting. The resemblance they both bear to typhoid fever in their symptoms has caused them to be regarded as the analogue in cattle of this malady; but their power of communicating this or any other disease to man is doubtful, and may be considered as still *sub judice*. The sale of such meat is, however, rightly stopped, because, even if incapable of conveying its specific contagion, it is undoubtedly much deteriorated in quality, and its nutritive power much diminished. The evidence against pleuro-pneumonia is much

stronger, as it is a distinctly contagious and febrile
disease, tainting the entire body of the animal
affected, and warranting its exclusion from the meat
market. Yet so inefficient is the working of the
legislation upon the subject that Dr. Carpenter, of
Croydon, mentions a recent instance of an outbreak
of pleuro-pneumonia in his district, in which it appeared in a farmyard among forty cows, which were
all in one shed. The local inspector isolated the first
cow, leaving thirty-nine in the shed in which the first
case appeared. Of these, twenty-two were seized
in about six weeks, one after the other, with the
disease, and were taken out of the shed, slaughtered,
and buried on the premises; but the rest of the herd
were killed by the owner and *used as food*, though
they had been kept the whole time in the infected
shed. Yet the inspector of the Local Government
Board had agreed that all proper steps had been
taken in this instance to prevent the spread of the
infection. Of course, if these cattle had been
examined at the market after being slaughtered, as
would have been the case if intended for Jewish food,
they would all have been condemned as unfit. Dr.
Cameron, the Medical Officer of Health for Dublin,
has given it as his opinion, confirmed by large experience and abundant evidence, that bad results
ensue from the consumption of this class of meat, yet
it continues to be sold at a cheap rate as food to the
poor.

Foot-and-mouth disease, the fourth on our list, has
been defined as "a contagious eruptive fever, affecting all warm-blooded animals and attacking man;"
and its whole history, during the long period in which

it has been prevalent on the Continent, and during the last forty years when this country has suffered so much from it, shows that it is indeed a malady of both man and beast. "The communication of the disease to man," says Gangee, one of the highest authorities, "admits of no doubt;" and Mr. Vacher, the Medical Officer of Health for Birkenhead, in a paper read at the Cambridge meeting, asserts very decidedly that if imperfectly cooked meat from an animal affected with this malady be eaten, it undoubtedly places the consumer within reach of infection.

The class of diseases of cattle known technically under the name of "Anthrax," of which there are several varieties, is certainly communicable to man by ingested flesh. The investigation of this question has been conducted chiefly by French and German physiologists, and they are unanimous as to the facility with which the malady can be conveyed as food, and as to its fatal character; indeed Mr. Vacher asserts that the tenacity with which the flesh of the affected animal retains the infection is so great, that it is impossible to assign a limit to it, or to the peril of the consumer.

In respect to erysipelas in cattle, the communication of the disease to man from infected food, though exceedingly probable, is scarcely capable of direct proof—because, firstly, the malady is quite as common in man as it is in animals; and, secondly, it occupies such a peculiar position between specific and simple diseases, that when an outbreak occurs, it is impossible to say whether it is due to contagion or not. It is, however, so frequently met with, especially in sheep and pigs, that the possibility of its

conveying its special infection should never be over-
looked, and it should be condemned as utterly unfit
for human food, especially as flesh scarcely showing
any physical signs of the disease may, nevertheless,
be found actively infective, owing to the insidious
manner in which the poison of erysipelas is conveyed.

Lastly, the chief interest of this enquiry centers
in the question of the communicability of tuberculosis
from animals to man, because not only is this class
of maladies the most destructive of all to which
human beings are liable (being accountable for at
least one-fifth of the entire mortality of the country),
but also because, though it was long a matter of
doubt whether the disease as it exists in cattle was
identical with that of man, this question has now
been solved in the affirmative; and the evidence of
the communicability of the disease is rapidly gaining
strength. It is only comparatively recently that the
suspicion of tubercle being conveyed to the consumers
of flesh so tainted has been entertained; but its in-
oculability is no longer a matter of dispute, and it has
been repeatedly proved that the malady can be produced by feeding with the flesh or milk of diseased
cattle. There is no doubt that thousands of animals
in this condition are slaughtered and sold for food,
and the only method of prevention recommended by
Mr. Fleming is the establishment of public *abattoirs*
throughout the country, the inspection of all carcases
about to be issued from them as food, and the con-
demnation and destruction of all such as are found
affected with this malady. It is indeed highly probable that much of the infantile scrofula and tubercle
so prevalent among all classes, and especially the

poor, is attributable to the consumption of the flesh and milk of tuberculous cattle. The prevalence of the disease among bovine animals is known to be very great, though, owing to the absence of sanitary inspection of cowsheds and slaughter-houses, it cannot be exactly estimated. But it appears to be largely on the increase, and on the Continent it has been ascertained that from one to five per cent. of all cattle are tuberculous. Animals thus affected do not, as a rule, show signs of wasting, and it is thus only by examination after death that its existence can be detected. I may add that the results arrived at on this subject by English physiologists have been abundantly confirmed by Continental physicians, among whom may be named Gerlach, Chauveaux, Colin, and many others, all of whom have shown that tubercle can be transmitted by the ingestion of the flesh and milk of diseased cattle.

The conclusion to be arrived at from a consideration of the entire subject are, that of the specific diseases of animals used as food, the parasitic, anthracoid, erysipelatous, tuberculous, and foot-and-mouth varieties may be deemed directly transmissible to man, that the question of the communicability of cattle-plague and swine-typhoid is as yet undetermined, and that the evidence as to pleuro-pneumonia, though much stronger, does not so far admit of absolute demonstration. Of course there is not a shadow of doubt that all such meat is not fit for human food, being deprived of most of its nutritive qualities; but this is a different question from the transmissibility of the identical and specific disease.

I am myself decidedly of opinion that the care

bestowed upon the examination of meat for the use of the Jewish community is an important factor in the longevity of the race, which is at present attracting so much attention; and in its comparative immunity from scrofula and tubercle, to which Dr. Gibbon, the Medical Officer of Health for Holborn, has so markedly alluded in his last report. Naturally such cases do not produce an immediate effect, but their transmission through innumerable generations must eventually bring about a decided result, and exercise a considerable influence in building up the mental and physical toughness of the Jewish people, which has been so long an object of wonder; and which, in conjunction with their steadfastness, cohesion and valor, Goethe considers to be their chief claim before the judgment-seat of nations.— *Dr. Henry Behrend, in the Jewish Chronicle.*

Medical and Scientific Testimony in favor of a Vegetarian Diet.

The Italics are not those of the Authors quoted, but are used to call attention to the more remarkable words or passages bearing upon the point in question. It is not implied that all the authorities mentioned are in favor of Vegetarianism, either in theory or practice. They are quoted to attest facts, rather than to enforce opinions.

PROFESSOR OWEN.—"The apes and the monkeys, which man nearly resembles in his dentition, derive their staple food from fruits, grain, the kernels of nuts, and other forms in which the most sapid and nutritious tissues of the vegetable kingdom are elab-

orated; and the close resemblance between the quad-
rumanous and human dentition shows that man was,
from the beginning, adapted to eat the fruit of the
trees of the garden."—*Odontography*, p. 471.

BARON CUVIER.—"The *natural* food of man, judg-
ing from his structure, appears to consist principally
of the fruits, roots, and other succulent parts of
vegetables."—*Animal Kingdom*, p. 46 (Orr, London,
1840.)

M. DAUBENTON.—"It is, then, highly probable
that man in a state of pure nature living in a confined
society, and in a genial climate,—where the earth
required but little culture to produce its fruits,—
did subsist upon these, without seeking to prey on
animals."—*Observations on Indigestion.*

M. GASSENDI.—"Wherefore, I repeat, that from
the primeval and spotless institution of our nature,
the teeth were destined to the mastication, *not of
flesh, but of fruits.*—*Works*, vol. x., p. 20.

LINNÆUS.—"This species of food [fruit] is that
which is most suitable to man; which is evinced by
the series of quadrupeds; analogy; wild men; apes;
the structure of the mouth, of the stomach, and the
hands."—*Linnæi Amœnitates Academicæ*, vol. x., p. 8.

RAY.—*Certainly man by nature was never made
to be a carnivorous animal,* nor is he armed at all for
prey or rapine, with jagged and pointed teeth, and
crooked claws sharpened to rend and tear; but with
gentle hands to gather fruit and vegetables, and with
teeth to chew and eat them."—*Evelyn's Acetaria*,
p. 170.

SIR HENRY THOMPSON, F.R.C.S.—"The vegetable eater, pure and simple, can extract from his
food all the principles necessary for the growth and
support of the body as well as for the production of
heat and force (p. 11). It must be admitted as a
fact beyond question, that some persons are stronger
and more healthy who live chiefly or altogether on
vegetables (p. 12). We have already seen that not
only can all that is necessary to the human body be
supplied by the vegetable kingdom solely, but that,
as a matter of fact, the world's population is, to a
large extent, supported by vegetable products.
Between forty and nearly sixty degrees of latitude,
we find large populations of fine races trained to be
the best laborers in the world on little more than
cereals and legumes, with milk (cheese and butter),
as food " (p. 26).—*Food and Feeding*.

DR. W. B. CARPENTER, C.B., F.R.S.—"There is
ample and unexceptionable evidence that where
neither milk nor any of its preparations is in ordinary
use, a regimen consisting of bread, fruits, and herbs
is quite adequate to the wants of a population sub-
sisting by severe and constant toil."

PROFESSOR LAWRENCE.—"The teeth of a man have
not the *slightest* resemblance to those of the carnivorous animals, except that their enamel is confined
to the external surface. He possesses, indeed, teeth
called ' canine '; but they do not exceed the level of
the others, and are obviously unsuited to the purposes which the corresponding teeth execute in carnivorous animals, - . . . Thus we find that,
whether we consider the teeth and jaws, or the

immediate instruments of digestion, the human structure closely resembles that of the simiæ; all of which, in their natural state, are completely herbivorous ".[frugivorous ?]—*Lectures on Physiology*, pp. 189, 191.

BELL.—"It is, I think, not going too far to say, that every fact connected with the human organization goes to prove that man was originally formed a frugivorous animal. . . . This opinion is principally derived from the formation of his teeth and digestive organs, as well as from the character of his skin; and the general structure of his limbs."—*Anatomy, Physiology, and Diseases of the Teeth.*

DR. SPENCER THOMPSON.—"No physiologist would dispute, with those who maintain that man ought to live on vegetables alone, the possibility of his doing so, or that many might not be as well or better under such a system as any other," etc.—*Dictionary of Domestic Medicine*, Art. 'Food.'

HALLER.—"This food, then, which I have hitherto described, and in which flesh has no part, is salutary; insomuch that it *fully nourishes* a man, protracts life to an advanced period, and prevents or cures such disorders as are attributable to the acrimony or grossness of the blood,"—*Elements of Physiology*, vol. vi., p. 199.

DR. G. CHEYNE.—"For those who are extremely broken down with chronic disease, I have found no other relief than a total abstinence from all animal food, and from all sorts of strong and fermented liquors. In about thirty years' practice, in which I have (in some degree or other) advised this method in proper cases, I have had but two cases in whose total recovery I have been mistaken."—(1709).

ARBUTHNOT.—"I know more than one instance of irascible passions being much subdued by a vegetable diet."

HUFELAND.—The more man follows Nature, and is obedient to her laws, the longer will he live; the further he deviates from these, the shorter will be his existence. . . Plain, simple food only, promotes moderation and longevity; while compounded and luxurious food shortens life. . . Instances of the greatest longevity are to be found among men who, from their youth, lived principally on vegetables, and who, perhaps, never tasted flesh."

LIEBIG.—Grain, and other nutritious vegetables, yield us, not only in starch, sugar, and gum, the carbon which protects our organs from the action of oxygen, and produces in the organism the heat which is essential to life, but also in the form of vegetable fibrine, albumen, and caseine, [the elements of] our blood, from which the other parts of our body are developed. . . . Vegetable fibrine and animal fibrine, vegetable albumen and animal albumen, hardly differ even in form; . . . and when they are present, the graminivorous animal obtains in its food the very same principles on the presence of which the nutrition of the carnivora entirely depends. . . . . Vegetables produce, in their organism, the blood [matter] of all animals; for the carnivora, in consuming the blood and flesh of the graminivora, consumes, strictly speaking, only the vegetable principles which have served for the nutrition of the latter."

DR. LANKESTER.—"Animal food is composed of the same materials as vegetable food. It is formed of the same elements, and presents the same proximate principles."—*Guide to the Food Collection*, p. 79.

MOLESCHOTT.—" The legumes are superior to meat in abundance of solid constituents which they contain; and while the amount of albuminous substances may surpass that in meat by one-half, the constituents of fat, and the salts, are also present in a greater abundance."

Society Reports.

THE VEGETARIAN SOCIETY, NEW YORK.
EXECUTIVE COMMITTEE FOR 1896.

President,   JOHN WALTER SCOTT.
First Vice-President,   MRS. M. A. HAVILAND.
Second Vice-President,   GEORGE BRUNSWICK.
Treasurer,   CHARLES A. MONTGOMERY.
Secretary,   ARTHUR HAVILAND.

Regular Meetings held on the fourth Wednesday in the month at 27 West 42nd street.

56TH REGULAR MEETING.

At the 56th meeting of the Vegetarian Society, New York, held at the Fifth Avenue Hall, on December 21, 1896, Vice-President Brunswick presiding and eleven members present, the topic announced was "The Byways of Vegetarianism," which the

Chairman explained to be the ways other people travelled in the pursuit of health and humanity, as *our* ways are evidently the highways towards those ends. This opened a discussion as to the errors in diet, which, with music by Miss Hamma, filled the evening pleasantly and instructively.

At a late meeting, Dr. Foote stated that "Character is a resultant of many influences. Food is one of the important ones, but hardly to be considered in advance of heredity. That is the first powerful factor that stamps its impress on every living thing. Next comes environment, which is a combination of several factors. Climate has, as Licky shows, been a large factor in shaping the character of peoples and destiny of nations. Food fairly deserves to be considered next, unless perhaps education deserves preference.

"The remark has been made by some experienced head of a public institution, that, if he could have entire control of the food of a man or a people, he could decide their character. He could, thereby, no doubt, do much, probably not all he claimed. We are called upon to remark the difference between herbivorous and carnivorous animals; the amiability of the former and natural ferocity of the latter, but, while true in the main, there are exceptions. Possibly the gorilla, in his family circle, is amiable, a loving husband, fond father and quiet citizen, but, as seen by strangers (to him), his ferocity equals that of the lion and tiger, and among the herbivorous feeders there is also the unamiable and untamable zebra.

"Coming to nations, it is true that those where vegetarian living predominates, the people are generally vigorous physically and placid mentally, but, as to the latter, perhaps the Irish might be named as an exception, and he who catches a fine Tartar, finds, if I mistake not, a man who eats almost no meat. The docility and controlability of Asiatics, whose subjection by carnivorous Europeans has been cited as evidence of the energetic qualities imparted by meat eating, have had their character formed by climate as well as by food, and by centuries of subjection to autocratic government.

"The progress toward civilization during the last few hundred years has been mainly among the meat-eating nations, and this fact has served as a standing argument for those who claim that such diet is essential to great activity, energy and progress, but, no nation has ever exhibited such remarkable ability and quickness in all movements of *present* civilization, of which, success in war seems to be the greatest element, as the Japanese: and, it would probably not be possible to show that their awakening and progress has been coincident with or dependant upon any considerable change in the dietetic habits of their teachers in the arts of war and manufacture.

"Food, therefore, cannot be regarded as the dominant influence in character building, and to determine its effects one must carefully observe differences in habits of people where 'other things are equal' in the main."

Names of two new members were proposed. The Society proposes to hold some of its meetings in the Y. M. C. A. building, 23rd street and 4th avenue.

A. HAVILAND, *Secretary.*

THE
Vegetarian·

SUBSCRIPTION:

Per Year, prepaid, to any part of the World, ... *25 cents.*
10 Subscriptions, to different addresses . . . . . *$1.00.*
Single copies, 2 cents; 50 cents per 100.

Published Monthly by
The Vegetarian Publishing Company, 40 John Street, New York City.

Entered at the New York Post Office as Second-class matter.

| VOL. II. | FEBRUARY 15, 1897. | No. 8. |

Plutarch—Essay On Flesh-Eating.

A. D. 40-120.

"You ask me upon what grounds Pythagoras abstained from feeding on the flesh of animals. I, for my part, marvel of what sort of feeling, mind, or reason, that man was possessed who was the first to pollute his mouth with gore, and to allow his lips to touch the flesh of a murdered being; who spread his table with the mangled forms of dead bodies, and claimed as his daily food what were but now beings endowed with movement, with perception, and with voice.

"How could his eyes endure the spectacle of the flayed and dismembered limbs? How could his sense of smell endure the horrid *effluvium?* How, I ask, was his taste not sickened by contact with festering wounds, with the pollution of corrupted blood and juices? 'The very hides began to creep, and the flesh, both roast and raw, groaned on the spits, and the slaughtered oxen were endowed, as it might seem, with human voice.' This is poetic fiction; but the actual feast of ordinary life is, of a truth, a veritable portent—that a human being should hunger after the flesh of oxen actually bellowing before him, and teach upon what parts one should feast, and lay down elaborate rules about joints and roastings and dishes. The first man who set the example of this savagery is the person to arraign; not, assuredly, that great mind which, in a later age, determined to have nothing to do with such horrors.

"For the wretches who first applied to flesh-eating may justly be alleged in excuse their utter resourcelessness and destitution, inasmuch as it was not to indulge in lawless desires, or amidst the superfluities of necessaries, for the pleasure of wanton indulgence in unnatural luxuries that they—the primeval peoples—betook themselves to carnivorous habits.

"If they could now assume consciousness and speech they might exclaim, 'O blest and God-loved men who live at this day! What a happy age in the world's history has fallen to *your* lot, you who plant and reap an inheritance of all good things which grow for you in ungrudging abundance! What rich harvest do you not gather in? What wealth from the plains, what innocent pleasures is it not in your power to reap from the rich vegetation surrounding you on all sides! *You* may indulge in luxurious food without staining your hands with innocent blood. While as for us wretches, *our* lot was cast in an age of the world the most savage and frightful conceivable. *We* were plunged into the midst of an all-prevailing and fatal want of the commonest necessaries of life from the period of the earth's first genesis, while yet the gross atmosphere of the globe hid the cheerful heavens from view, while the stars were yet wrapped in a dense and gloomy mist of fiery vapors, and the sun [earth] itself had no firm and regular course. Our globe was then a savage and uncultivated wilderness, perpetually overwhelmed with the floods of the disorderly rivers, abounding in shapeless and impenetrable morasses and forests. Not for us the gathering in of domesticated fruits; no mechanical instrument of any kind wherewith to fight against nature. Famines gave us no time, nor could there be any periods of seed-time and harvest.

"What wonder, then, if, contrary to nature, we had recourse to the flesh of living beings, when all our other means of subsistence consisted in wild corn [or a sort of grass], and the bark of trees, and even slimy mud, and when we deemed ourselves fortunate to find some chance wild root or herb? When we tasted an acorn or beech-nut we danced with grateful joy around the tree, hailing it as our bounteous mother and nurse. Such was the gala-feast of those primeval days, when the whole earth was one universal scene of passion and violence, engendered by the struggle for the very means of existence.

"'But what struggle for existence, or what goading madness has incited *you* to imbrue your hands in blood—you who have, we repeat, a superabundance of all the necessaries and comforts of existence? Why do you belie the ground as though it were unable to feed and nourish you? Why do you do despite to the bounteous [goddess] Mother Earth, and blaspheme the sweet and mellow gifts of Dionysius, as though you received not a sufficiency from them?

" 'Does it not shame you to mingle murder and blood with their beneficent fruits? Other *carnivora* you call savage and ferocious—lions and tigers and serpents—while yourselves come behind them in no species of barbarity. And yet for them murder is the only means of sustenance; whereas to you it is a superfluous luxury and crime.'

" For, in point of fact, we do not kill and eat lions and wolves, as we might do in self-defence—on the contrary, we leave them unmolested; and yet the innocent and the domesticated and helpless and unprovided with weapons of offence—these we hunt and kill, whom nature seems to have brought into existence for their beauty and gracefulness. . . .

" Nothing puts us out of countenance, not the charming beauty of their form, not the plaintive sweetness of their voice or cry, not their mental intelligence, not the purity of their diet, not superiority of understanding. For the sake of a part of their flesh only we deprive them of the glorious light of the sun—of the life for which they were born. The plaintive cries they utter we affect to take to be meaningless, whereas, in fact, they are entreaties and supplications and prayers addressed to us by each which say 'It is not the satisfaction of your real necessities we deprecate, but the wanton indulgence of your appetites. Kill to eat, if you must or will, but do not slay me that you may feed *luxuriously.'*

" Alas for our savage inhumanity! It is a terrible thing to see the table of rich men decked out by those layers out of corpses, the butchers and cooks: a still more terrible sight is the same table *after* the feast—for the wasted relics are even more than the consumption. These victims, then, have given up their lives uselessly. At other times, from mere niggardliness, the host will grudge to distribute his dishes, and yet he grudged not to deprive innocent beings of their existence!

" Well, I have taken away the excuse of those who allege they have the authority and sanction of nature. For that man is not, by nature, carnivorous is proved, in the first place, by the external frame of his body—seeing that to none of the animals designed for living on flesh has the human body any resemblance. He has no curved beak, no sharp talons and claws, no pointed teeth, no intense power of stomach or heat of blood which might help him to masticate and digest the gross and tough flesh-substance. On the contrary, by the smoothness of his teeth, the small capacity of his mouth, the softness of his tongue and the sluggishness of his digestive apparatus, Nature sternly forbids him to feed on flesh.

" If, in spite of all this, you still affirm that you were intended by nature for such a diet, then, to begin with, kill *yourself* what you wish to eat—but do it yourself with your own *natural* weapons, without the use of butcher's knife, or axe, or club. No; as the wolves and lions and bears themselves slay all they feed on, so, in like manner, do you kill the cow or ox with a gripe of your jaws, or the pig with your teeth, or a hare or a lamb by falling upon and rending them there and then. Having gone through all these preliminaries, *then* sit down to your repast. If, however, you wait until the living and intelligent existence be deprived of life, and if it would disgust you to have to rend out the heart and shed the life-blood of your victim, why, I ask, in the very face of Nature, and in despite of her, do you feed on beings endowed with sentient life? But more than this— not even after your victims have been killed will you eat them just as they are from the slaughter-house. You boil, roast, and altogether metamorphose them by fire and condiments. You entirely alter and disguise the murdered animal by the use of ten thousand sweet herbs and spices, that your natural taste may be deceived and be prepared to take the unnatural food. A proper and witty rebuke was that of the Spartan who bought a fish and gave it to his cook to dress. When the latter asked for butter, and olive oil, and vinegar, he replied, 'Why, if I had all these things I should not have bought the fish!'

"To such a degree do we make luxuries of bloodshed, that we call flesh 'a delicacy,' and forthwith require delicate sauces for this same flesh-meat, and mix together oil and wine and honey and pickle and vinegar and all the spices of Syria and Arabia—for all the world as though we were embalming a human corpse. After all these heterogenous articles have been mixed and dissolved and, in a manner corrupted, it is for the stomach, forsooth, to masticate and assimilate them—if it can. And although this may be, for the time, accomplished, the natural sequence is a variety of diseases, produced by imperfect digestion and repletion.

"Diogenes (the Cynic) had the courage, on one occasion, to swallow a *polypus* without any cooking preparation, to dispense with the time and trouble expended in the kitchen. In the presence of a numerous concourse of priests and others unwrapped the morsel from his tattered cloak, and putting it to his lips 'For your sakes,' cried he 'I perform this extravagant action and incur this danger.' A self-sacrifice truly meritorious! Not like Pelopidas, for the freedom of Thebes, or like Harmodius and Aristogeiton, on behalf of the citizens of Athens, did the philosopher submit to this hazardous experiment, for *he* acted thus that he might *unbarbarize*, if possible, the life of human kind.

"Flesh-eating is not unnatural to our physical constitution only. The mind and intellect are made gross by gorging and repletion; for flesh-meat and wine may possible tend to give robustness to the body, but it gives only feebleness to the mind. Not to incur the resentment of the prize-fighters [the *athletes*], I will avail myself of examples nearer home. The wits of Athens, it is well known, bestow on us Bœotians the epithets 'gross,' 'dull-brained,' and 'stupid,' chiefly on account of our gross feeding. We are even called 'hogs.' Menander nicknames us the 'jaw-people.' Pindar has it that 'mind is a very secondary consideration with them.' 'A fine understanding of clouded brilliancy' is the ironical phrase of Herakleitus. . . . .

"Besides and beyond all these reasons, does it not seem admirable to foster habits of philanthropy? Who that is so kindly and gently disposed towards beings of another species would ever be inclined to do injury to his own kind? I remember in conversation hearing, as a saying of Xenokrates, that the

Athenians imposed a penalty upon a man for flaying a sheep alive, and he who tortures a living being is little worse (it seems to me) than he who needlessly deprives of life and murders outright. We have, it appears, clearer perceptions of what is contrary to propriety and custom than of what is contrary to nature.

"Reason proves both by our thoughts and our desires that we are (comparatively) new to the reeking feasts of kreophagy. Yet it is hard, as says Cato, to argue with stomachs that have no ears; and the inebriating potion of Custom has been drunk, like Circe's, with all its deceptions and witcheries. Now that men are saturated and penetrated, as it were, with love of pleasure, it is no easy task to attempt to pluck out from their bodies the flesh-baited hook. Well would it be if, as the people of Egypt, turning their back to the pure light of day, disembowelled their dead and cast away the offal, as the very source and origin of their sins, we, too, in like manner, were to eradicate bloodshed and gluttony from ourselves and purify the remainder of our lives. If the irreproachable diet be impossible to any by reason of inveterate habit, at least let them devour their flesh as driven to it by hunger, not in luxurious wantonness, but with feelings of shame. Slay your victim, but at least do so with feelings of pity and pain, not with callous heedlessness and with torture. For it is sufficiently evident that men have indulged their lawless appetites in the pleasures of luxury, not for necessary food, and from no necessity, but only out of wantonness, and gluttony, and display."—[*From " The Catena of Authorities Denunciatory and Deprecatory of the Practice of Flesh-eating." By Howard Williams, M.A.*]

Sir Isaac Pitman.

We regret to have to chronicle the death of Sir Isaac Pitman, the inventor of stenography and one of the best known vegetarians in England.

Isaac Pitman was born at Trowbridge, Wilts, on January 4, 1813. After six years' service as a clothier's clerk he was sent to the Normal College of the British and Foreign School Society, London, and after five months' training, at the close of 1831 he was appointed master of the British School, Barton-on-Humber. He established the British School at Wotton-under-Edge in 1836, and removed to Bath in 1839. His first treatise on shorthand, entitled "Stenographic Soundhand," appeared in 1837. He devoted his entire attention to spelling reform and his system of phonetic shorthand after 1843, when the Phonetic Society was established. His system of shorthand was renamed in 1840 and entitled "Phonography."

His "Phonographic Reporter's Companion" appeared in 1846. Mr. Pitman edited and printed the *Phonetic Journal.* Besides printing his own instruction books for teaching phonetic shorthand, Mr. Pitman issued a library of about eighty volumes, printed entirely in shorthand, ranging from the Bible to "Rasselas." An international shorthand congress was held in London in the autumn of 1887, and a gold medal from the phonographers of the United States and one from those of Great Britain and the Colonies were presented to Mr. Pitman in recognition of his labors for the reformation of English orthography. Mr. Pitman was knighted in 1894.

It will be noted that hard work when supported by a rational diet has no evil effect on the human frame. Sir Isaac lived and worked for over eighty-four years before he entered into rest.

The following letter written by Pitman in 1879 is a good tribute to the value of vegetarianism as a mode of life independent of its moral value. We reprint in the vernacular as it might be troublesome reading to those unacquainted with Sir Isaac's system. " Sir:—

" A friend suggests to me that I ought to write a letter to the *Times*, placing my life experience in contrast with the editorial summing-up on Mr. W. Gibson-Ward's vegetarian letter in the *Times* of last Thursday. The conclusion arrived at is: ' So long as no special call is to be made on the strength, a purely vegetable diet may suffice.' As my life has been one of exceptional activity, the fact that is has been maintained on a vegetable diet ought to be known, now that a discussion on diet has been admitted into the the *Times*.

" My dietetic experience is simply this : About forty years ago dyspepsia was carrying me to the grave. Medical advisers recommended animal food three times a day, instead of once, and a glass of wine. On this regimen I was nothing bettered, but rather grew worse. I avoided the meat and wine, gradually recovered my digestive power and have never since known, by any pain, that I have a stomach.

" These forty years have been spent in continuous labor in connection with the invention and propagation of my system of phonetic shorthand and phonetic spelling, correspondence, and the editorial duties of my weekly journal. Though sixty-five years of age, I continue the custom I have followed all through this period, of being at my office at six in the morning, summer and winter. Till I was fifty years of age, I never took a holiday, or felt that I wanted one; and for about twenty years in the first part of this period I was at my desk fourteen hours a day, from six in the morning till ten at night, with two hours out for meals. Twenty years ago I began to leave off at six in the evening.

"I attribute my health and power of endurance to abstinence from flesh meat and alcoholic drinks. I can come to no other conclusion when I see the effect of such extended hours of labor on other men who eat meat and drink wine or beer. I have written my letter phonetically, as is my custom, and shall feel obliged if it be allowed thus to appear in the *Times*.

Isaac Pitman.

Phonetic Institute, Bath, January 27, 1879.

India's Pestilence.

Although we advocate vegetarianism solely on the ground of right, we are always pleased to be able to prove that it is also best: that it insures health, strength, happiness and long life; that it will in time cure most diseases, and makes its strict followers immune from the attack of the various contagious maladies which carry off such a large portion of the human race who die in childhood or in the prime of life. Indeed, it is very doubtful if sickness ever entered the world until the inhabitants had forsaken the food that was so abundantly provided for them and commenced to prey on animals and one another, thus placing themselves on a par with the lowest class of animal life, for it must be noted that all the higher order of animals subsist entirely on vegetable food.

We have before us the report of Dr. Cantlie on the pestilence now raging in India, from which we extract the following:

"All flesh-eating animals are affected by the plague, above all the rat, while none of the purely herbivorous animals is attacked. Of course," says Dr. Cantlie, "the rabbit, guinea pig, and a number of animals can be inoculated experimentally or made to consume plague disease food, but no herbivorous animal acquires it by the natural processes of infection. If it is by consumption of flesh that animals are infected, how do human beings get it? The animals affected seem to become infected from flesh; the snake from the rat, the jackal, pig and dog from eating the flesh of persons dead from plague: but how does the rat become infected? Could we find that out we should likely know how man is infected."

A Plea For Singing Birds.

I am ashamed to say that one night at dinner I ate a thrush. It was the first, it shall be the last, of God's feathered musicians put to so bad a use. I awoke in the early hours of the morning with the beautiful dead and devoured songster on my conscience, and these were my reflections: Five-and-twenty people, each of them capable of pleasure from its song, transmuting that enjoyment into the vulgar gratification of making a mouthful of the singer.

When we see a cat stalking a blackbird we instinctively interpose and rescue the bird; when we read of a tiger eating a man we are thrilled with horror. Think of a lion eating Livingstone! as seemed likely to be his fate; but God delivered him. Could such a man be put to a more ignoble use? But neither the cat, the tiger, nor the lion knows any better; they eat, unconscious of iniquity. But for a man to eat a nightingale, or a lark, or a linnet! how contemptible.

Think of the beautiful words which God has given men to write concerning these minstrels of the heavens. Imagine our great poet listening to the song at heaven's gate—"Hark, the Lark at heaven's gate sings," and then sitting down to a dish of larks!

Think of Hogg's breezy address to the same sweet singer—

"Bird of the wilderness,
Blithesome and cumberless,
Sweet be thy matin o'er moorland and lea;
Emblem of happiness
Blest be thy dwelling place,
O to abide in the desert with thee!"

To think of eating the creatures that God created to make music in the trees and in the air, to keep us mindful of our lost paradise, and to woo us to our home above! The prophets and sweet singers of Israel owed something to the voice of the turtle, the mourning of the dove; how much do we owe to the music in the atmosphere which poets have translated into words. R. COPE MORGAN.

Society Reports.

THE VEGETARIAN SOCIETY, NEW YORK.
EXECUTIVE COMMITTEE FOR 1896.

President,　　　　　　　JOHN WALTER SCOTT.
First Vice-President,　　MRS. M. A. HAVILAND.
Second Vice-President,　GEORGE BRUNSWICK.
Treasurer,　　　　　　　CHARLES A. MONTGOMERY.
Secretary,　　　　　　　ARTHUR HAVILAND.

Regular Meetings held on the fourth Tuesday in the month at 98 Fifth avenue.

57TH REGULAR MEETING.

At the 57th meeting of the Vegetarian Society, New York, held at 98 Fifth avenue, on January 26, 1897, President Scott in the chair, nine members and three visitors present, the minutes of the last meeting were read and approved.

A vote of thanks to the publisher of THE VEGETARIAN was passed, tendering to him the congratulations of the Society upon the good work done.

The Committee on Publication stated they had had printed one thousand postal cards for the use of the Secretary and had procured a number of copies of "*Perfect Way in Diet,*" which were being circulated among friends.

Committee on Restaurants called attention to a restaurant at 222 Sixth avenue, where vegetarians would find good food.

Mr. Spencer stated his belief to be that one should eat freely of those parts of plants containing the germinating principle, as cereals, nuts, seeds, etc.,

without milling, cooking, or other destructive operation.

Mr. Montgomery spoke of the plans of work proposed by Mr. Perkey, President of the Cereal Machine Co., which would be of great benefit to the
cause of food reform.

Antonio Bastida, 119 East 23d street, and Mrs.
Sarah L. Emory, 18 Broadway, were elected members.

The names of Mrs. J. Rhinhart, 257 Fourth avenue,
and Mrs. Michand, 15 East 9th street, were proposed
as associates.

It was moved that the election of officers for the
ensuing year, postponed from the Annual Meeting,
in November, be the next business.

It was moved by Miss Hamma, seconded by Mr.
Spencer, that the persons now holding the offices of
this Society, be elected to fill the same respectively
for the coming year.   Carried.

It was moved and carried that the present com-
mittees be continued until their successors be
appointed.

Miss Hamma was appointed a member of the
Committee on Restaurants, vice Miss Ohlmeyer

It was stated that among the many full notices of
the life of Sir Isaac Pitman lately deceased, only one,
the *Evening Sun* of January 22, stated the fact of
his practical Vegetarianism.

It was moved that the Treasurer arrange with the
janitor for the rental of Room 5, 98 Fifth Avenue,
for the use of this Society on the 4th Tuesday of
each month to the June meeting.

Adjourned.   A. HAVILAND.

THE VEGETARIAN·

SUBSCRIPTION:

Per Year, prepaid, to any part of the World, ... 25 cents.
10 Subscriptions, to different addresses . . . . . $1.00.
Single copies, 2 cents; 50 cents per 100.

Published Monthly by
The Vegetarian Publishing Company, 40 John Street, New York City.

Entered at the New York Post Office as Second-class matter.

VOL. II.   MARCH 15, 1897.   No. 9.

War and Reason.

BY COUNT LEO TOLSTOI.

In the year 1896 a young Dutchman named Van Der Ver was summoned to enter the National Guard. The summons of the commander was answered by Van der Ver in the following letter :

"THOU SHALT NOT KILL."

To M. Herrmann Sneiders, Commander of the National Guard in the district of Midelburg.

"HONORED SIR:—Last week I received a letter in which I was commanded to appear at the town hall in order to be enrolled in the National Guard in accordance with the law. As you may have noticed I did not appear, and it is the object of this letter to inform you, openly and simply, that I do not intend to appear before the Commission. I know quite well that in taking this step I incur a heavy responsibility,

that you can punish me for it, and that you will not
fail to do so. But this causes me no anxiety. The
reasons which compel me to remain passive afford
me a sufficient counterpoise to this responsibility.

"Although I am not a Christian, I understand better
than most Christians the command which I have written
at the beginning of this letter, the command which
agrees alike with human nature and with reason.
When I was a child I permitted people to teach me
the handiwork of soldiers, the art of murdering.
Now I refuse. I have no desire to murder at the
word of command. This would be to murder against
my conscience, and without any personal motive.
Can you tell me of anything which is more degrading
to a human being than the carrying out of such murders and slaughter? I can neither commit murder
myself nor can I bear to see a brute slaughtered. In
order that no animal may be killed on my account I
have become a vegetarian. In the case in point I
can be ordered to shoot people who have never done
me any harm; I do not believe that soldiers learn to
shoot simply at the leaves and branches of trees.

"But you will perhaps reply that the National
Guard, before all else, serves for the protection of
order in the land.

"Sir, if order really reigned in society, if the social organism were really healthy, if no abuses could
be found in our social relations crying to heaven for
redress, if it were not permitted that one dies from
hunger while another enjoys every whim of luxury
—yes, then you would see me in the vanguard of the
defenders of order. But I refuse to support the
maintenance of the present so-called order. Why

throw sand in one's own eyes? Both of us know
quite well what it is to support this order. It means
the support of the rich against the working poor,
who are now beginning to recognize their right.
Have we not seen the *role* which your National
Guards played in the last strike in Rotterdam, when
those soldiers stood for hours to protect the goods of
firms which were threatened? And can you believe
for one minute that I would consent to defend people
who, according to my firm conviction, are only sup-
porting the battle of labor and capital, that I would
consent to shoot down workers who are well within
the bounds of their rights? You cannot be so blind.
Why make the affair more complicated? I really
cannot permit you to educate me to become an obedient National Guardsman.

"For these reasons, but especially because I hate
murder at the word of command, I refuse to enter
the service of the National Guard, and beg you to
send me neither uniform nor arms, as I have the un-
alterable intention not to use them.

"J. K. VAN DER VER."

In my opinion this letter possesses a very deep
meaning. Objections to render military services
have appeared in Christian States since the time when
military service first existed, or, more accurately
stated, since the time when the States, whose
power rests on force, accepted Christianity without
freeing themselves from the use of force.

Of real Christians there have always been only a
few. The great majority of the men in Christian
States are reckoned Christians because they confess
the church faith, which is, however, only in name

identical with true Christianity.   The fact that now
and then one of the tens of thousands who rendered
military service has objected has not influenced in
the least those millions who annually serve.

"But it is impossible that that monstrous multitude
of Christians who render such service should be in
error, and that only the exceptions have right on
their side—exceptions many of them men of inferior
culture, while archbishops and scholars explain how
military service is not in antagonism to Christianity."
So say the vast majority of people, and, continuing
to believe themselves Christians, they enter the ranks
of the murderers.

But here comes a man, not a Christian, as he himself says, and objects to render military service, not
from religious, but from the most simple considerations which concern every one and which every one
of every confession and nationality can appreciate—
be he Catholic, Mohamedan, Buddhist, Confucian,
Spaniard, Arab or Japanese.

Had Van der Ver given as reason for his refusal
the fact that he belonged to some particular Christian body, those who are approaching military service
might say, "I belong to no sect, and do not confess
Christianity, and therefore I need not act as he acted."
But Van der Ver's principles are so simple, so clear,
and so applicable to every one that we must take them
to ourselves.   If we do not, then we must say,' I love
murder, and am ready to kill, not only the enemy, but
also my own oppressed and unfortunate fellow-
countrymen, and see nothing heinous in the obligation
to kill all those whom my commander for the time
being orders me to kill."

And yet everything is so clear.

The young man lives. No matter in what position or in what confession he grows up, he is taught to be good, and that it is bad not only to kill a man, but to beat and kill an animal. He is taught that a man must treasure highly his moral worth, and that this moral character consists in acting in accordance with his conscience. This is taught him, whether he is a Chinese Confucian, a Japanese Shinto or Buddhist, or a Turkish Mohamedan; and then, as soon as all this has been explained to him, he enters military service, where the exact contrary is demanded from him. He is commanded to prepare himself not merely to kill and wound animals but men. He is freed from his idea about moral worth, and taught the business of murdering unknown men. To this demand, what can a man of our time reply? Only this, "I will not and can not do it."

Van der Ver did this. And it is hard to say what else he and others in his position could answer.

It is possible that a man may exist who does not think of what he is doing when he enters military service. Perhaps there are still men who wish war with other nations and still further suppression of workmen: who love murder for its own sake. Such people may be warriors, but even these must know that there are those, the best people in the universe, not only among Christians, but among Mohamedans, Brahmins, Buddhists and Confucians who contend against and hate war and militarism, and that their number increases with every hour. No arguments can subvert the simple truth that a man who respects himself can be the slave of an unknown or even known master with murderous intentions. And this is the essence of military service and its discipline.

"But you forget the responsibility incurred by those who will not serve. It is all very well to preach martyrdom. You are old. You are secure through your position. You will not be subjected to this trial. But how about those to whom you preach, who trust you, and in refusing to serve ruin their young lives?"

"Yes, but what shall I do?" I reply to people who say this. Because I am old, shall I, therefore, desist from pointing out that evil which I recognize as clear? I am old, I have lived long and thought much. Let us take, as an example, a robber on the bank of a river who wishes to compel one man to murder another. Should I refrain from crying, "Hold your hand," because I am on the other side of the river and cannot be touched by the robber, or because my interference in all probability will only excite him still more? Besides, I do not see why the Government, which persecutes those who refuse to serve, should not punish me from whom they have learned their ideas. I am not so old that I cannot be persecuted and punished, and as to my position that is no protection. At any rate, whether I am persecuted or not, those will be condemned and punished who refuse to serve, and therefore so long as I live I shall not cease to say what I am now saying. I cannot cease to act as my conscience prescribes.

The power and invincibility of Christianity consists in this, that in order to become powerful among men it requires no support from outside. Whether one is old or young, persecuted or not, if you have assimilated the Christian or the true view of life you cannot recede from the demands of your conscience. Therein consists the essence and peculiarity of Christianity when compared with all other religious teachings. Therein lies its invincible power.

As a fire on the steppe or in the forest burns until it has consumed all that is dry, withered and burnable, so will a truth once expressed in words, work and work until it has destroyed the whole lie which girdles and conceals the truth. The fire smoulders for a long time, but as soon as it breaks out all that can be burned is consumed. So with the idea which cannot find expression, let it but find clear expression in words and the evil and the lie speedily succumb. One of the private utterances of Christianity—the idea that humanity can exist without slavery, existed and was accepted in Christianity, but it found no intelligible expression before the time of the writers who lived at the close of the eighteenth century. Until this time not only were the old pagans, Plato and Aristotle, unable to conceive of human society without slavery, but other people as well, Christians, who are nearer us.

Thomas More could not conceive his Utopia without slavery. In the same way at the beginning of this century it was impossible for men to think of the life of humanity without war. It was only after the Napoleonic wars that the thought that men could live without war was clearly uttered. Hardly one-hundred years elapsed after the utterance of the idea that men could live without slavery and slavery had ceased to exist among Christians, and in nothing like another hundred years war will have ceased to exist. It is quite possible that war will not be completely abolished, just as slavery has not been completely abolished. It is quite possible that military force will continue to exist just as the wages system continues to exist after the abolition of slavery, but neither will war nor the army assume that shape so repugnant to reason and moral feeling which it has at present.

And numerous signs indicate that this time is near. These signs are seen in the confused condition of governments who are perpetually increasing their armaments, in the ever increasing weight of the burdens of taxation, in the discontent of the people, in the terrible deadliness of artillery, in the activity of peace societies and congresses; but above all, in the refusal of single persons to serve. In this refusal lies the key to the solution of the question.

Every recognition of the truth—or better expressed, every liberation from any error, as in the case of slavery—will always be productive of a hard battle between the consciousness of men and the attraction of former conditions.

At first the attraction is so strong and the consciousness so weak that the first attempt to liberate from error is only greeted with shakings of the head. The new truth is stigmatized as nonsense. "Can we live without slavery? Who will work then? Can we live without carrying on war? Everyone will come and conquer us." But the power of conscience rises, attraction weakens, and in place of the headshaking we have mockery and contempt. "The Holy Scriptures recognize lord and servant. Such relations have always existed. And now wise people have been found who will turn the whole world upside down." This was the way slavery was spoken of. "Scholars and philosophers have recognized the legality and even the sanctity of war, and now we are suddenly asked to believe that it is no longer necessary to conduct war!" This is the manner in which war was spoken of. But the conscience of man rises, and the view gets clearer; the number of those who recognize the new truth gets greater and ever greater, and in place of the mockery and contempt we get cunning and deceit. Those who support the error make it appear that they are alive to the unreasonableness and the cruelty of those measures which they defend, but contend that their abolition at this particular time is impossible, and postpone the matter to some future time. "Who does not recognize the wickedness of slavery, but men are not yet ripe for freedom, and their liberation would entail great misfortune." So they said more than forty years ago about slavery. "We all see that war is an evil; but so long as men so closely resemble beasts the abolition of the army will bring about more evil than good." People speak now of war in this way. Still, the idea is doing its work; it grows, and the lie is being consumed. The time is coming when the unreason, aimlessness, injuriousness and immorality of the error will be so apparent that it will be no longer defended. This was seen during the sixties in Russia and America with regard to slavery. And this is the position of affairs now with reference to the conduct of wars. Just as at that time no attempt was made to justify slavery, so now is the existence of war and army not justified. It only wants a drop of water to trickle through the embankment, or a single

brick to fall out of the building, or a single mesh of
the net to unravel, and the embankment collapses,
the building falls and the net goes in two. Such a
drop of water, brick or mesh is the action of Van der
Ver. Other refusals must follow that of Van der
Ver, and in increasing numbers, and as soon as the
number is large enough those very persons, and
their name is legion, who yesterday said that it was
impossible to do without war will say that they have
long preached against its immorality and unreasonableness, and advise you to act as Van der Ver has
acted, so that from war and army in the form in
which they now exist only a recollection will remain.
And this time is near.—*The Christian World.*

Reviews.

*The Vegetarian, 19 Memorial Hall, Farringdon
street, London, England.*

We are not reviewing ourselves, as might be supposed by the heading, but a larger, and we sincerely
hope, a better work of the same name. It is better
because it comes once a week instead of once a
month and therefore should be productive of more
good. We recollect when soon after our paper was
started it was objected to on the ground that there
already was a *Vegetarian* in the field; we replied that
we were glad to hear it and trusted that before long
there would be a vegetarian paper published in every
city of the world.

The paper before us consists of sixteen large
pages and cover and is published at one penny a
week; from the style of it we should say that it was

principally sold on stands and in book stores as we do not note any special notice of yearly rates, but we have no doubt but that a dollar bill will secure it for a year and we earnestly advise all our readers to subscribe; you cannot get too many vegetarian papers and should you get more than you can read give them to your friends, thus accomplishing two good deeds—helping to support papers that certainly require the help of every vegetarian, and doing your share to spread a knowledge of the truth.

The Unconscious Holocaust.

By J. Howard Moore.
Author of Why I am a Vegetarian.

There is nothing more frightful to the philosopher than the unconscious tragedies of human reason. Men are somnambulists. Stupified by the long night of instinct out of which it arose, the human mind is only half awake to the world of reality and duty. George Washington was the father of his country and a great and good man, but he held human beings as slaves and paid his hired help in Virginia whiskey. It took Americans one hundred years to find out that "all men" includes Ethiopians. Men who risk their lives in order to achieve personal and political liberty for black men deliberately doom white wonen to a similar servitude. A rich man will give millions of dollars to a museum or a university, when he would know, if he had the talent to stop and think, that the thousands who make his wealth, work like wretches from morning till night and feed on garbage and suffocate in garrets, in order that he may be munificent.

But, without doubt, the most frightful inconsistency of civilized minds to-day is seen in the treatment accorded by human beings to their sub-human associates. Human nature is nowhere so hideous and the human conscience is nowhere so profoundly asleep as in their ruthless disregard for the life and happiness of the non-human animal world. It is enough almost to make villains weep—the cold-blooded manner in which we cut their throats, dash out their brains and discuss their flavor at our cannibalistic feasts. As Plutarch says, "lions, tigers and serpents we call savage and ferocious, yet we ourselves come behind them in no species of barbarity." From our cradle up we have been taught that mercy to the lamb and the heifer is a disease, and we have become so accustomed to deeds of violence and assassination that we perpetrate them and see them perpetrated without the semblance of a shudder.

See that dainty lady going down the aisles of the cathedral! She looks in her silks and loveliness the very picture of purity and innocence. But look closer, and you will discern in her faultless art the disfigurement of crime. See those furs! They did not fall like snowflakes from the bounteous lap of heaven. They were stripped from the quivering form of some outraged northern creature to whom life and happiness were as dear as to her. Look at her head-dress! Those fluttering wings are the remains of song-birds whose beauty and joy once filled the woods and fields. But their throats were silenced and their beautiful and happy lives ended forever to

amuse the vanity of this spiced and be-ribboned wor-
shipper. She ate breakfast this morning, and she ate
that which compelled the darkest crime on the cal-
endar—murder! Her innocence, therefore, is in the
eyes of those who behold her, and her conscience is
spotless only because she is asleep.

And so with us all—we are criminals—criminals of
the most shocking hue. And if we were only able to
shake off this somnambulism and see ourselves as we
are and as the future will certainly see us, we would
be terrified by the crimes we are committing. Take
the delicate organism of the heifer—an organism
more beautiful and in some respects more tender
and wonderful than that of human beings. We will
take that sensitive organism, all palpitating with life
and full of nerves, and torture it and mutilate it and
chop it into twitching fragments with a composure
and nonchalance that would do honor to the man-
agers of an inferno. We call ourselves the paragons
of the universe, yet we are so hideous and inhuman
that all other beings flee from our approach as from
a pestilence. We preach the Golden Rule with an
enthusiasm that is well-nigh vehement, and then
freckle the globe with huge murder-houses for the
expeditious destruction of those who have as good a
right to live as we have. Every holiday is an occasion for special massacre and brutality. Thanksgiving, the day above all others when it seems men's
minds would be bent on compassion, is a furious
farce. Instead of being a day of grace, mercy and
peace, it is a day of gluttony and ferocity. Killing
tournaments by "crack shots" are the order of the
day. Imprisoned pigeons, suddenly freed, are shot

down without mercy by unfailing marksmen. In
many places rival squads of armed men scour forest
and prairie, indiscriminately massacreing every living creature that is not able to escape them, and for
no higher or humaner purpose than just to see which
side can kill the most! This is a crime unparalleled
on the face of the earth. No-species of animal, except man, plunges to such depths of atrocity. It is
bad enough in all conscience for one being to send a
bullet through the brain of another in order to tear
it to pieces and swallow it, but when such outrages
are perpetrated by organized packs just for pastime,
it becomes an enormity beyond characterization!

Look at the scenes to be met with in all our great
cities! They are enough to horrify a heart of flint!
An army of butchers standing in blood ankle deep
and working themselves to exhaustion cutting the
throats of their helpless fellows—unsuspecting oxen
with limpid eyes looking up at the deadly pole-axe
and a moment later lying a-quiver under its relent-
less thud—struggling swine swinging by their hinders
with their life leaping from their gashed jugulars—
an atmosphere in perpetual churn with the groans
and yells of the massacred—streets thronged with
unprocessioned funerals—everywhere corpses dang-
ling from salehooks or sprawling on chopping-blocks
—men and women kneeling nightly by their pillow
sides and congratulating themselves on their white-
ness and rising each morning and leaping on the
bloody remains of some slaughtered creature—such
are the spectacles in all our streets and stock yards,
and such are the enormities perpetrated day after
day by Christian cannibals on the defenceless dumb
ones of this world!

It is simply monstrous—this horrible savagery and somnambulism in which we grope. It is the climax of mundane infamy—the "paragon of the universe"(?) dozing on the pedestal of his imagination and contemplating himself as an interstellar pet and all other beings as commodities. Let us startle ourselves, those of us who can, to a realization of the holocaust we are perpetrating on our feathered and fur-covered friends. For remember the same sentiment of sympathy and fraternity that broke the black man's manacles and is to-day melting the white woman's chains will to-morrow emancipate the sorrel horse and the heifer, and as the ages bloom and the great wheels of the centuries grind on, all the races of the earth shall become kind and this age of ours, so bigoted and raw, shall be remembered in history as an age of insanity, somnambulism and blood.

The Vegetarian Society, New York.

We much regret that the report of last month's meeting of the above society has not yet reached our office, so after waiting three days we are compelled to go to press without it. This is especially to be regretted as the last meeting was a very interesting one, several new speakers having addressed the assembly.

The next regular meeting will be held on Tuesday, March 23, at 98 Fifth avenue.

All are invited to attend.

THE VEGETARIAN·

SUBSCRIPTION:

Per Year, prepaid, to any part of the World, ... 25 cents.
10 Subscriptions, to different addresses . . . . . . $1.00.
Single copies, 2 cents; 50 cents per 100.

Published Monthly by
The Vegetarian Publishing Company, 40 John Street, New York City.

Entered at the New York Post Office as Second-class matter.

VOL. II.   APRIL 15, 1897.   No. 10.

The Vegetarian.

It is some time since we have had a word to say about ourselves and perhaps our remarks have been long since forgotten so it may not be out of place to call attention to our hopes and aims.

THE VEGETARIAN is published monthly to help in the great cause of civilizing the world.

The price is low so that every poor person can subscribe, and it is offered at cost of paper and sewing, by the hundred, so that it can be freely given away by all possessed of any means.

The size is small so that it can be folded in half and enclosed in an ordinary envelope.

Each paper is practically an essay by itself appealing in turn to every noble impulse of the human heart, so that our friends may be enabled to select some one number which exactly expresses their views. This can be bought by the thousand and given away.

We have no sympathy with the vegetarian who

finds that he has discovered a good thing; a system of living which enables him to reduce his expenditure, increase his working capacity, enjoy perfect health and look forward with certainty to long life, thereby securing a great advantage over his fellow workers, and then keeps his good fortune to himself.

Vegetarianism is not good because it insures all these blessings, but because it unites us in bonds of love and sympathy with all created beings, be they higher or lower in the scale of life than ourselves.

THE VEGETARIAN makes no claim to originality. It deems it a crime to use inferior language to convey an idea that has been better expressed by others. It freely takes all that it finds good in the works of others, giving due credit therefor, and offers all of its best to all, with or without acknowledgement.

THE VEGETARIAN has no axes to grind. No desire to make money, not even to pay expenses, but simply to do the greatest possible good with the means at the disposal of its publishers.

THE VEGETARIAN does not set itself up as a standard, or advocate its claims to the exclusion of other papers on the same subject. It freely advertises all that is good in vegetarian literature and advises its readers to buy, according to their means, every paper published advocating "on earth peace, good will towards men "—and animals.

If you can help to support it we think it your duty to do so according to your means. If you cannot afford to buy it many of our readers will be glad to pay for it for you.

If there is any number which you think specially appropriate for any public meeting we will forward free of charge, and if out of print, reprint for the occasion.

The Ethics of Diet.

Being an address delivered in Gilfillan Memorial Church, Dundee, on Sunday, February 28, 1897.

By Albert Broadbent.

I have an unpopular message to deliver to you this evening, and will ask you to listen to it in the spirit of Philippians iv. 8.

"Whatsoever things are true, whatsoever things are honorable, whatsoever things are just, whatsoever things are pure, whatsoever things are lovely, whatsoever things are of good report: Brethren, think on these things."

I wish that my address to you might be as beautiful as the words I have just asked you to keep in mind.

I have been generously permitted by your kind and broad-minded pastor to address you on a matter of deep concern to me, the subject of the Ethics of Diet.

The dictionary rendering of the word Ethics is, that it is the science of moral duty, a system of rules for regulating the actions of men, and I desire to talk with you on the regulation of our actions in things relating to diet.

I am sure there is no need that I should apologize for introducing such a subject in this church, and on this day. It has not been forgotten by the pastor and the members of this church at any rate, that religion claims the body as well as the soul. Pure food makes pure blood, pure blood a healthy body.

The healthier the body, the healthier and less sickly our religion will be; and if there is any truth in the German proverb—"that as a man eats, so is he," it may be assumed that mentally, physically and morally, we are influenced by the food we eat. Doubtless but few of us worshipping here this evening have thought that the science of ethics might be applied to our eating. And yet there is an ethical way of eating, in line and agreement with St. Paul's beautiful words, true, honorable, just, pure, lovely, and of good report, a plan of eating which may be associated with life's *blameless things*.

Everywhere around us we feel there is a movement towards fuller and more worthy life, true men and women are striving to win for others, less privileged, the chance of living the better life; a desire to bring the time of which William Watson sings in his poem in the *Daily Chronicle* last week. I quote one verse—

"Fiercely sweet as stormy springs,
    Mighty hopes are blowing wide;
Passionate prefigurings,
    Of a world revivified.
Dawning thoughts that ere they set
Shall possess the ages yet."

There are many present here who have seen words like these come true, and who have also seen many a social wrong, ignobly die. And many social evils these days are trembling, for the ferment is in the air. And one of the first evils to go will be the spirit of war; even now we see and feel the time that is coming.

And then, dear friends, I yearn with passionate

longings for a time that shall be, but is not yet, when another war shall have ceased, when our British nation shall be redeemed from another blot that, in the eyes of Easterns, now sullies her fair name.

The time when we shall have ceased to *make war upon animals*, and to slaughter them for human food.

Is there then urgent need of reform in things relating to our food? There is great need, because by our present eating customs is much cruelty caused to animals, fishermen, fishes and birds.

Mention might be made of the sufferings of rail and sea-borne cattle, the cruelties of drovers, the horrors of slaughter-houses, the boiling of living lobsters, skinning of eels, crimping of cod, the eating of shell fish alive. The fearful loss of life in our fishing industries: it is stated that five hundred fishermen lose their lives annually in this trade, and the greater part of the year are exposed to bitter cold. Even birds are not excepted from this cruelty and oppression, this spirit of war. The manufacture of *Pate de foi gras* causes much cruelty to geese—the birds used for this purpose have the food crammed down their throats, and are kept cooped up in small wooden boxes away from the light with legs tied, and are stuffed and packed with food to make their livers grow inordinately, to supply the sated appetites of European epicures.

A species of this same cruelty has come to Britain, and in many of our agricultural centers are now dotted here and there poultry farms, where birds are fed by machinery, and cooped up in small boxes to fatten them quickly for the London and provincial markets.

How woful, how saddening to think of so much
cruelty associated with our food, food to many of our
minds seemingly needful for the nourishment of our
bodies.

Do we ever ask whence the ordination of these
things, these sufferings caused to our lower brethren?
Has God ordained it? our hearts answer *no*, we think
of Him as *tender*, loving, gentle and desiring not the
death of any creature.   He has not ordained it, but
yet permits it, the evil is of man's ordaining.   "Love
is God's essence," says Philip Bailey, and love delights not in sorrow and suffering.

The feeling which has grown more and more upon
me is that these customs are all wrong, because unnecessary.   Once I did not feel this way, but one
day I began to think of it all and conscience became
a very tyrant, until the determination came to leave
these customs behind; now my position is like that
of the man whom Christ healed, and made to see,
and who, when questioned about the miracle that
had been wrought upon him, said, "Once I was
blind, now I see."   And many of us are blind to the
cruelty about us because we do not permit ourselves
to think of it.

Far be it from me to assume a spirit of self-right-
eousness or superiority in presenting these thoughts
to you on a subject about which I have so deep concern.   Flesh eaten as food contains no wondrous
magic force, as food it is only valuable for the chemical elements it contains, and these same properties
are found abundant in the foods that come direct
from the fruit and vegetable world; fruits, nuts,
cereals, pulses and vegetables are quite sufficient for

the body's needs, and being sufficient for nourishment, to my mind, they make flesh-eating unnecessary, and the cruelty thereby caused wrong.

Shelley held that to kill animals and eat their flesh was to break Nature's law, and that she avenged herself by sowing in the bodies of men the germs of disease and misery.

We all know that much harm comes to us through the use of the flesh of animals as food.

I hope I shall have succeeded in helping you to see that the Science of Ethics—a system of morals—may be applied even to such a commonplace thing as eating.

If we can lessen pain or suffering in the lives of those around us, it is our duty as sincere Christians so to do, to have our garments clean of stain in these things. Let us be content to leave animals to Nature, to stop breeding them, and cease to feel that we can only keep them in place, and sustain the balance of nature by eating them.

Many of us are seeking to enjoy healthier and happier lives, let us seek it Nature's way. I am glad to be able to tell you that I have seen many a foul disease go its way before the power of a simple and pure diet.

How we long and search to find the way to health, wearily we toil and spend and search, but wrongly. My friends, the way to health is a simple and easy one to go, it is like the way to Heaven that Scripture tells us, "Is so simple that a wayfaring man, though a fool in other things, need not err therein."

But this way lies not over a path bestrewn with physic bottles, pill boxes, and patent foods, but by eating pure food, breathing pure air, and observing cleanliness.

I take much comfort often when I think of some who have gone this way. The singers of undying songs, men who have left behind them "thoughts that breathe and words that burn." The founders of the literature of the present day, who in times of sated luxury and ease, preserved the power to think and sing by living the simple life. Such men as Plato, Plutarch, Socrates, Ovid, Pythagoras, Seneca, Hesiod, and a host of others.

Since I began to live this way there has come into my life much peace and tranquility, now as I take my humble meal, I can dwell on every detail of its production with pleasure and gladness, because it comes through gentle and kindly ways. How different from the olden days, when it used to be a labor to try and forget the sufferings of the animals. And now I see the truth in Wordsworth's beautiful words where he implores us—

"Never to blend our pleasure or our pride
    With sorrow of the meanest thing that feels."
With Coleridge that—
    "He prayeth well, who loveth well,
        Both man and bird and beast.
    He prayeth best, who loveth well,
        All things both great and small.
    For the dear Lord who loveth us,
        He made and loveth all."
Sings Emily Dickenson—
    "If I can stop one heart from breaking
        I shall not live in vain.
    If I can ease one life the aching, or cool one pain,

Or help one fainting robin,
I shall not live in vain."

And this more ethical way tends to lessen the pain and suffering in the world.

My mind will sometimes travel back to the time of which King David tells:—"When the morning stars sang together, and all the angels of God shouted for joy." The time called in the first chapter of Genesis, "the beginning," where the food of man is spoken of, and it is that of which I make choice, and it is said of it, "that it was very good."

Closing—as I began—in the spirit of charity and kindliness, I leave these few thoughts with you, in Paul's words asking that—

"Whatsoever things are true, whatsoever things are honorable, whatsoever things are just, whatsoever things are pure, whatsoever things are lovely, whatsoever things are of good report: Brethren, think on these things."—*The Vegetarian, London.*

C. H. Sorley.

The friends of vegetarianism will learn with sorrow of the death of C. H. Sorley, President of the Chicago Society. He died in what should be the prime of life for a vegetarian, in his seventieth year, a comparatively young man, for no one expects a pure liver to die before he has at least passed his eightieth birthday.

The loss to our ranks is a severe one, as our departed friend was an entertaining writer and a fluent expounder of the practice and doctrine of vegetarians and was so situated that he was enabled to devote a large part of his time to the spread of the reform he had so close to his heart. Mr. Sorley has long been suffering with an incurable disease and it was solely owing to his vegetarian diet that he was enabled to withstand its ravages so long.

The last few days of his existence were embittered by the conduct of an unnatural son, who, we are informed, took advantage of the weakened condition of his parent and forced him to pollute his body with various flesh products, which probably did much to hasten his death.

Many persons were surprised to find a sensational notice of Mr. Sorley's death published in practically every paper in the United States, and many comments were made and inquiries instituted as to what great influence could have been exerted to secure such widespread publicity to a simple family bereavement.

We are now informed that Mr. Sorley's son is in the employ of Armour & Co., the Chicago slaughterers. All honor to our departed friend, for in his life he must have cut heavily into the unholy profits of the multi-millionaire pig sticker, to have induced him to spend the sum of money necessary to secure such wide publicity to the death of a simple vegetarian. The day has gone by when people can be frightened into returning to the disgusting food they have discarded, by the announcement that at last they have learned of the death of a vegetarian who died before he reached his hundredth birthday. The fiendish howl of exultation will do more harm than good. Were we inclined to be personal we could point out the fearful effects of a flesh diet in those who are near and dear to this fearful butcher, if such a feeling is possible in a slaughterman.

Recipes.

MACARONI SOUP.—Half a pound of Naples macaroni, one quart of mushrooms, two turnips, one onion, three Jerusalem artichokes, one dessert-spoonful of potato-flour, quarter of a pint of cream, and four ounces of bread crumbs. Boil the macaroni in two quarts of water, with a teaspoonful of salt and a small piece of butter. When tender, drain the water from it; wash it in fresh water, lay it in a clean cloth for a short time, and cut it in pieces about an inch in length. Wash the mushrooms without paring them or cutting off the stems; put them in a pan with three quarts of water—the turnips, onions, artichokes, bread crumbs, mace, pepper and salt; boil them till the vegetables are perfectly soft, rub them through a sieve, return the soup into the pan, put in the macaroni, set it on the fire again, stir in the potato-flour, mixed with a little cold water, till quite smooth; add a little cayenne pepper and salt as required; and when it has boiled ten minutes add the cream.

SEAKALE.—The short, thick kale is the best. Trim it nicely, and tie it in bundles. Boil it in plenty of water, with two ounces of salt. When tender, drain it in a clean cloth; lay it neatly in a dish upon toasted bread, which should be previously dipped in the water, and serve with butter sauce.

Society Reports.

THE VEGETARIAN SOCIETY, NEW YORK.
EXECUTIVE COMMITTEE FOR 1896.

President,	JOHN WALTER SCOTT.
First Vice-President,	MRS. M. A. HAVILAND.
Second Vice-President,	GEORGE BRUNSWICK.
Treasurer,	CHARLES A. MONTGOMERY.
Secretary,	ARTHUR HAVILAND.

Regular Meetings held on the fourth Tuesday in the month at 98 Fifth avenue.

58TH REGULAR MEETING.

At the 58th meeting of the Vegetarian Society, New York, held February 23, at their new Hall, 98 Fifth avenue, the president being in the chair and eleven members and twenty-three visitors present, the minutes of the last meeting having been read the election to membership of Mrs. Rhinhard and Mrs. Michand was announced.

Mr. C. A. Montgomery, in discussing the topic "Aggressive Vegetarianism," stated that there were five duties we owed to the cause: join a society, pay the dues, attend meetings, distribute literature, and exert a personal influence.

Judge Hemiup, President of the Vegetarian Society of Minneapolis, said that food reform was at the bottom of and the inspiration of *all* reforms. He saw before him thirty vegetarians surrounded by a population of two millions—a truly small center of influence—yet, they may be doing more than is apparent. The beginnings of all enterprises of reform are small. The world is sick, society is sick—surfeited with rich food. As to his personal experience, he said that at the age of forty, thirty-eight years ago, he noticed incipient symptoms of old age; he read works on " Longevity," became a vegetarian and endeavored to approach nearer to nature's suggestion of food. Women are the power of the movement. In the Minneapolis Society, six women and two men had signed the articles of the Society, then they had a banquet and in two months their number was doubled, for they approached the problem with enthusiasm, and had used the press and printing freely. "Let us do all we can; let us become students, so that we can give reasons for the faith that is in us. The sickness of the world is due to the fact that the world has used animal food for generations—the craving for it is a matter of heredity. How much can we do to eliminate this appetite from us and our children?"

Mr. L. A. Goodaine, late of New Orleans, stated that he stumbled across vegetarianism. In May, 1896, he was very ill; physicians gave him up; death surely would occur within a week, as he was suffering from affections of the lungs, heart and kidneys. He took his case into his own hands, stopped medication and ate freely of fruits, his only food. In less than a week he felt better and his strength rapidly increased. He has maintained that system of diet ever since, and he is now stronger than ever.

Mr. Deihl read a paper on Vegetarianism, and the Society adjourned.

A. HAVILAND, *Secretary.*

59TH REGULAR MEETING.

At the 59th meeting of the Vegetarian Society, New York, held at their Hall, 98 Fifth avenue, on Tuesday, March 23, 1897, President Scott in the chair and Dr. Holbrook, the Countess Wachtmeister and fifty-five others present, the reading of the minutes of the last meeting was, on motion of Mr. Montgomery, omitted.

The Countess Wachtmeister, who with Mrs. Annie Besant is making a tour of the world in the interest of the Theosophical Society, was introduced to speak upon "Vegetarianism in the light of Theosophy." She stated she had been a vegetarian for seventeen years; it was necessary to be such for she leads a life of hard work with much travelling, using for the past six months, while traveling, a diet of fruits, nuts and brown bread.

"In the constitution of man there are four distinct bodies: the physical, which should be considered as a temple for the dwelling of the soul, and hence it is our duty to keep it clean and pure by the use of grains and fruits; the astral, which is fed by the psychical emanations of our food, it is therefore necessary to eat fruits and grains which ripen in the sunlight; the mental, which is fed on thoughts we assimilate as our own; the spiritual, which is the body of light taken into the heavenly state and is fed on spiritual thoughts.

"There are many reasons why we should be vegetarians.

"Meat eaters are liable to disease.

"The growth of vegetarianism in England is

almost incredible; there are so many restaurants with customers waiting, and it seems that the more restaurants there are in London the more they are filled.

"It is true that no vegetarians have been found in prison, in the workhouse, nor drunk.

"Theosophists consider it wrong to take life, therefore they eat only fruits, cereals, etc., in which life is latent, but without blood.

"It is awful to eat flesh when we consider the frightful amount of agony endured in a city to supply the meat. If every man were his own butcher, every one would be a vegetarian.

"Agony of animals before slaughter produced irritation to their psychic nature and that effects the nature of those who eat their flesh.

"Flesh is a stimulant, while the vegetarian's diet nourishes. Evolution goes on and our bodies grow of a finer nature.

"Many try to be vegetarians but fail, thinking they must eat vegetables only. This is not a sufficiently nutritious diet. The animal within you craves for meat, and for a few weeks there is an intense desire for flesh. Treat the case naturally— make the change gradually and soon the craving for flesh will cease."

Dr. M. L. Holbrook read a paper upon "A Balanced Diet," which will be printed in full in the next issue of his *Journal of Health.*

Judge N. H. Hemiup and others made remarks upon the increase of the movement of food reform and urged the audience to help it along.

Adjourned. A. HAVILAND, *Secretary.*

The Vegetarian.

Volume I., attractively bound in linen, 236 pages, price $1.00

Contains many valuable articles on the subject and would make a suitable present for Vegetarians or thinking people.

THE PERFECT WAY IN DIET.

A treatise advocating a return to the natural and ancient food of our race.

—BY—

ANNA KINGSFORD,

Doctor of Medicine of the Faculty of Paris,

Sixth Edition, 1895.   Price $1.00, Post Free.

THE VEGETARIAN PUBLISHING CO., 40 John St., New York.

THE VEGETARIAN·

SUBSCRIPTION:

Per Year, prepaid, to any part of the World, ... 25 cents.
10 Subscriptions, to different addresses . . . . . $1.00.
Single copies, 2 cents; 50 cents per 100.

Published Monthly by

The Vegetarian Publishing Company, 40 John Street, New York City.

Entered at the New York Post Office as Second-class matter.

VOL. II.　　　MAY 15, 1897.　　　NO. 11.

Health.

BY E. G. DAY, M. D.

Read before the Vegetarian Society, New York, April 27, 1897.

We may define the word health as the state of being hale, sound, or whole in body, mind and soul and consider it in its three aspects. Let us then view the subject—if you please—as a triangle the three sides of which bearing, respectively, the words physical, mental and spiritual, embrace in close relation the one word health. As a triangle could not exist with one angle absent so a correct idea of health cannot be formulated with one of these principles missing.

We may then say that health consists of three principles, or aspects, physical health, mental health and spiritual health. Now in order that this unit may be perfect its components must be correlating and in equilibrium.

An excess or diminution in either impairs the integrity and perfectness of the whole.

We occasionally meet with persons in whom one of the aspects of health is abnormally emphasized.

In such instances the remaining two principles seem notably weakened. We may have seen individuals whose ambition was to attain to a high state of physical health with extreme muscular development.

These persons have but little taste for higher culture and ignore everything pertaining to the psychic or supersensuous, preferably "men of brawn" rather than "men of brains;" or, we may have met others who, intensely devoted to mental culture, have neglected the physical aspect of health and exhibited an undeveloped physique: the pale face, narrow chest, stooping shoulders and dragging step taking the place of those opposite conditions which suggest a vigorous physical body. There is indeed, at times, a prevalent air of disorder and bodily neglect about them unpleasant to witness; or we may encounter others who, floating away in mystical realms and striving to penetrate within the veil of the unseen, unwisely neglect to cultivate those mental and physical graces which render them fit and desirable companions. Only when equilibrium and harmony prevail between the physical, mental and spiritual do we view the *complete embodiment* of the principle we are now considering. Your attention is invited first to *Physical* health. I trust you will pardon the emphasis which may be laid upon this part of my subject and my very practical way of treating it. Behind the stomach, in front of the abdominal aorta —the great artery which conveys the blood to all the viscera, and the lower extremities—lies a large net-work of nerves and nerve ganglia, or knots from which branches extend to nearly every part of the body. Its anatomical name is the "Solar Plexus," from its divergent branches which radiate from a center analogous to the sun's rays. It has been called the "abdominal brain" as it seems to be the seat of a sub-conscious intelligence.

Its branches extend to all the vital organs, control and modify the processes of digestion, assimilation, absorption and elimination and through connecting channels extend to those nerves which proceed from the brain and spinal cord.

It is this great center which *presides over all* the *emotions* and plays an important role in the realm of dreams. Certain physical and mental conditions which are usually referred to the *heart* originate in the "solar plexus." The heart, anatomically consid-ered, is simply a double acting "force pump" which keeps the vital fluid in circulation through the blood channels by the rythmical contraction of its muscular walls and the action of its four valves in response to the nerves within its substance which are in direct connection with the solar plexus.

The "solar plexus" and not the heart is the seat of the affections, and their antithesis the baser passion. As this nerve plexus is in intimate relation with the *stomach* it happens that any abnormal condition of the latter organ seriously affects the functions of the former.

When we realize that seventy-five per cent. of human ailments originate in the stomach, it becomes obvious that a normal condition of the digestive organ is essential to the physical welfare of the individual.

As man is obliged to function through his body on this plane, his mental and spiritual health depend much upon an unimpaired physical condition, equally depends his physical well-being upon a normal mental state. It would be difficult to conceive of a chronic dyspeptic as a broad theologian or an advanced scientist. Similarly, one whose mental or spiritual health was impaired would not enforce those hygienic rules so essential to a sound physical body. The effects of a neuralgia or slight pulmonary lesion would be minor compared to the diffused influence of a diseased stomach, this organ being, as we have seen, in intimate relation with the "solar plexus," that great center of the "sympathatic nerve" system presiding over all the functions of the animal body. Little argument is needed to establish the importance of keeping the food receptacle in a healthy state. The stomach is lined with a delicate membrane which is studded with glands and traversed by nerves. These glands supply the digestive fluid of the body and upon their functioning properly, digestion depends. This digestive act is a process of reduction whereby the coarse particles swallowed are dissolved in the gastric juice. To facilitate this action the muscular walls of the stomach keep its contents in continuous motion. We unconsciously illustrate this process when we stir our tea or coffee to dissolve the sugar. Now as muscular action is by nerve incitation, it appears that a person with an impaired nervous condition might have a digestive organ which would fail to function properly, causing that sensation commonly described as a weight in the stomach. Every housewife recognizes that if she wishes to dissolve borax or soda rapidly she must pulverize it, but how few persons realize that the solubility of the food largely depends upon the thoroughness with which it is masticated. After the nutriment has been digested it passes as chyme into the small intestine—a tube about twenty feet in length—where the wonderful processes of separation, appropriation and absorption occurs. All the substances which are to repair the complex animal body are taken up by the capillaries—minute blood vessels which surround the lacteal or chyle vessels on the walls of the intestines. It is here that the *potential* energy locked up in the food is released and converted into *actual* energy and conveyed to the various parts of the body where it manifests as *physical* and mental activity. The small intestine terminates in the colon or large intestine, which may well be compared to a waste pipe, by which the unappropriated portion of the food is conveyed from the body. Important organs lie in close relation with the stomach, *viz.:* the liver, pancreas and spleen. Normal activity, which is essential to good health, a condition not to be expected if the former organ is diseased. The kidneys are important eliminators of waste material from the body. I am not able to understand why these glands from animals are so esteemed as food by many, as they are entirely excrementations and frequently diseased.

Some of the waste products pass off through the lungs as $C\frac{O}{2}$| and about one-third is eliminated by the skin as insensible perspiration. Through the lungs the blood receives *oxygen* which is conveyed by the microscopic red blood corpuscles—"the little oxygen wagons"—through the action of the great force pump, the heart, to *all* parts of the system. Upon this supply of *oxygen* all the varied manifestations of life depend. That our houses may be warmed, or that a steam engine may work, certain factors are requisite, *viz.:* fuel, a place for combustion, a good draft, and a smoke flue which serves the two-fold purpose of creating a draft and conveying away the unappropriated products of combustion. Why? Because in the fuel is stored potential—or possible—energy, in past ages it derived from the *sun*, which can be released only by burning or oxidation. It must be consumed in an appropriate place, otherwise the heat energy would be diffused into space and not utilized. A draft is requisite as it is by this means the oxygen passes in and supports combustion. A smoke flue is necessary, otherwise the deleterious products of imperfect oxidation would not be removed.

Every housekeeper and engineer know by daily experience that if the furnace is crowded with fuel and the draft left closed there will be no fire; that although the fire is properly fed and the damper open, no better results will be obtained if the smoke pipe is clogged; and still further, that although the furnace is intelligently operated, if the fuel is poor the desired result will be but partially reached.

Hence the necessity for good fuel. Again, with

all the above conditions fulfilled, if the fire is not systematically freed from ashes and these removed the machine will in time become inoperative. Now, this furnace represents the human body, for in each, certain processes are nearly *identical*. In our bodies we literally *burn* food to release the energy stored therein, and, that good results may follow, certain conditions are requisite, *viz.:* suitable food, plenty of oxygen and a free exit for all deleterious products of the animal oxidation. Let us consider first the fuel. The housekeeper prudently fills his bins with *good* coal to be burned in his simple cast iron furnace, but thoughtlessly supplies his larder with a conglomerate of food stuffs widely varying in quality and digestibility to be consumed in his complex and delicate body. Did the housekeeper or manufacturer attempt to heat his house or run his factory with the refuse of his kitchen he would excite reasonable doubts as to his sanity, but he can make a waste receptacle of his complex digestive apparatus without endangering his claim to intelligence and good judgment, and deluge his internal anatomy with a heterogenous mass of whiskey, wine, brandy, porter, tea, coffee, soda water, ginger ale, root beer, punch, milk and buttermilk combined with an indiscriminate assortment of solids ad libitum, expecting thereby to maintain the life fire long and bright. Many persons attend to their own heating apparatus and before retiring add a few shovels of clean coal to their fire knowing that it will enhance their personal comfort during the night. This duty discharged how many visit their pantries and stoke the internal furnace with, say, a slice of cold roast or boiled beef, or a tempting spare rib, or a portion of a fowl, or their inquisitive eyes detect some chicken or lobster salad left over from dinner which is at once appropriated. Possibly a section of mince pie may fall into line and be accompanied on its *dolorous* journey by a bit of cheese, and further temptation may be aroused by the silver sheen of the sardine or the variegated hue of the bologna. As gastronomic activity awakens thirst relief is sought in a draught of milk—an excellent but jealous food—or a bottle of the universal *lager*. They now seek their chambers, maybe, to commune with, their "higher nature" will positively decline to be interviewed, or to meditate on the varied and complex problems which daily engage the human mind. Hopelessly they wander round the outer walls of the subjects, entrance to the inner courts being denied. Finally "wrapping the drapery of the couch about them" they lie down to *troubled* dreams, awake with an indescribable flavor in the mouth, and wonder that they do not feel "just right."

Some one may exclaim "this is only ordinary food," and though we may limit our furnace to one variety of food, we cannot so restrict our stomachs. True, but we can care for our food receptacle as well as our fire box, and no more abuse the delicate walls of one than the fire brick surface of the other. If we crowd ourselves with the mass of food represented by an ordinary menu, not mentioning what would be a "chef d'œuvre" of a dinner or supper, we release agencies which ultimately must injure the abused organ, but if we demand only reasonable work, on a imited and judiciously selected supply of food, we will excite that healthy action which will benefit the entire body. The question arises naturally, what shall we eat? I would answer it advisory, not dogmatically, from my own experience. Let our diet be of those articles which within the least substance contain the most nutriment, and are easily digested.

Substitute for meat, in which fat, fibre and gristle predominate, the nutritious leguminous soups. Let the variety of vegetables be according to taste, not omitting the tender leaflets of lettuce, the crisp cress and the tender celery. Such relishes as "mixed pickles" and "chow-chow" may, with wisdom, be omitted. Potatoes agree with the majority, but the amount of starch they contain excludes them from the diet of some persons. Butter, of the best quality only, is nutritious when moderately used. Oysters in variety are esteemed as food, they being of a low order of life and to an extent self-digesting. Their conquerer, the clam, when young, is thought desirable. The lobster and its kindred are better left in their native element. The fact that creatures so forbidding in appearance are edible must have been discovered by some castaway. *Fish* possess but little value as food. The idea, long entertained, that it is a brain food, through its phosphoric element, is being relegated to the realm of the non-proven. If eaten, it should be very fresh as the flesh decomposes rapidly after death. The egg is one of two so-called perfect foods, and may be eaten in all ways except *raw;* if fried, it is best prepared with butter or olive oil. The objection to the raw egg is based on the fact that one of the metamorphoses of the "tape worm" has repeatedly been found in its substance. *All* animal substances, if eaten, should be subjected to at least *boiling* temperature before being eaten, to destroy the parasite and disease germs which lurk in the tissues. For this reason I regard a favorite food known as "*scraped beef*" (frequently prescribed for invalids) as dangerous.

The great variety of *cereals* should be used with moderation and discrimination, as they contain starch in excess, which, in some instances, promotes dyspepsia. The enticing hot roll, or smoking corn cake and muffin, the irresistible *waffle* coated with butter, garnished with sugar or floating in syrup are best taken at long intervals. The staple article of bread is, I think, best prepared from the *whole wheat* flour. In my opinion the very best articles of food are the sweet *fruits* and *nuts ready served* by nature. The idea that these two classes constitute mans' *natural food* is rapidly growing. These articles are rich in the carbonaceous and nitrogenous elements, the two most important ingredients in our food. Of these foods the finest and freshest alone should come to our tables. Among nuts I prefer the English walnut and pecan, especially the latter. I have found them very digestible, strengthening and satisfying, and patients for whom I have prescribed them have had similar experiences. The nut is fond of priority; if invited in at the end of the feast after a great assembly of foods have been entertained, it may prove rebellious, but when accorded a fair degree of prominence it behaves decorously. Among fruits the *apple* heads the list and may be eaten with every meal. Chemically, the apple is composed of vegetable fibre, albumen, sugar, gum, chlorophyl, malic acid, gallic acid, lime and much water. Further-more, the apple contains a larger percentage of phos-phorous than any other fruit or vegetable. The phosphorous is admirably adapted for renewing the essential nervous matter, *lecithin*, of the brain and spinal cord. The acids of the apple are of signal use for men of sedentary habits, whose livers are sluggish in action, as they serve to eliminate noxious matters from the body, which, if retained, would make the brain heavy and dull or bring about jaun-dice or skin eruptions and other allied troubles. Sweet *oranges* are appetizing and healthy when prop-erly eaten. *Bananas*, I am aware, are debatable; my own experience with this fruit has been most favorable and they are always on my table. The *date* is full of nutriment and forms a desirable break-fast dish (recipe). The *raisin* is a storehouse of energy awaiting release; the delicious pulp should alone be eaten. I believe that ripe, fresh fruit of all kinds may be eaten with benefit if taken at proper times and in a suitable manner, but I must warn you against mixing them with the miscellaneous food of an ordinary menu.

For beverages, *water* stands first. It is the great natural solvent of nearly all the substances which enter the animal body. It has been styled, not inappropriately, "Adam's Ale," as it is the great beverage which nature gave to the entire animal kingdom. It was flowing from countless fountains when man made his appearance on this planet. As a solvent for the food, or a quencher of the thirst it is never improved by any admixture. It may be taken freely at *normal temperature* whenever desired.

A glass of cold or hot water drank in the morning washes out the stomach, refreshes the intestinal tract and alleviates that unpleasant condition which is the prime cause of so many ills. *Milk* is the second perfect food in nature and contains everything required by the animal body, but only an infant up to two years of age can take enough to meet its physical requirements. As before stated, it is a jealous food, *ie.*, it serves best when taken alone. It frequently rebels against mixed society (sterilization). Tea, the cup which cheers but not inebriates, is to be regarded somewhat as a luxury and used accordingly. While it may at times be beneficial, the fact that it promotes indigestion must not be disregarded. It contains *tannin*—an active astringent—and is apt to make young persons appear prematurely old. In regard to *coffee*, I recognize the existence of different opinions concerning its value as a beverage. Personally I have not found it deleterious, though I do not now use it. The best preparations of chocolate and cocoa are harmless. All the *distilled spirits*, fermented and malt liquors may be put aside. Man —in my opinion—needs them no more, for beverages, than do the lower animals. Alcohol impairs the membranous lining of the stomach and thus interferes with digestion. Chronic gastritis of an aggravated type afflicts persons addicted to an immoderate use of alcoholic drinks. Alcohol *lowers* the temperature of the animal body, contracts the capillaries, impairs vitality and clouds the intellect. There are certain pathological conditions best known to the physician, which invite and justify its administrations, and where it partially atones for its demoniacal work under all other conditions. That vast quantities of *lager beer* and its kindred are annually consumed by invalids under the erroneous idea that benefit will result, is a fact full of appalling interest. The sole nutritive principle in the beer is the *malt*. The bitter principle, which is a slight appetizer, should come from the *hop*, but too frequently arises from a virulent poison. It is better to obtain the fine "extract of malt," as prepared by reliable chemical houses; put a teaspoonful into a tumbler and add a spray of vichy or seltzer. The combination is at once refreshing and strengthening. Beer and its congeners distend the stomach and intestines, producing that *corpulency* which is alike distasteful to men and abhorrent to women.

A similar condition results from over-crowding the system with food, or by eating those combinations from which fermentation results with the release of gasses. These cause dilation of the stomach, ultimately producing dyspepsia, and in the intestines induce corpulency. As those who are not vegetarians may be surprised that I have excluded *meat* from the dietary before referred to it becomes my duty to state my reasons for so doing. 1st.—The instant that an animal dies disintegration commences; this means, in plain terms, decomposition, putrefaction. Our senses cannot detect when this process has passed the "danger line." The rapidity of this process depends not alone on temperature, but on the physical condition of the animal before it was killed, and the manner in which its life was extinguished. 2nd.—The animal body is frequently the abode of *parasites* and disease germs which do not

die with the victim, but renew their activity in the
human organism.   This is proved by the history of
the "trichina" and the "tape worm," and those
formidable diseases which have been traced to the
animal tissues.   The fact that a multitude of *tuberculous* beeves are annually condemned and destroyed
suggests a disagreeable possibility.   3rd.—Meat contains much *scrap* which is not assimilated and demands abnormal activity in the human laboratory to
eliminate.   Organs which are overtaxed, in time,
lose their executive ability.   4th.—The continuous,
and especially the excessive use of animal flesh as
food, retards the growth of man's "higher" or
spiritual nature.   Man, having attained a human in-
carnation, is gradually eliminating the purely animal
elements, preparatory to the efflorescence and fruit-
age of his spiritual nature.   This, it is thought, may
be hastened by excluding from the system those cells
which made up the animal body and from which it
derived its vitality and nature.   The hypothesis is
worthy our attention.   5th.—It is not necessary as a
food; the important elements which it is supposed to
contain may be found elsewhere, especially in eggs,
milk, fruit and nuts.   Lastly, and principally.—The
killing of animals for food is a cruel and wanton sacrifice of that high, sensitive and sacred life which
comes from God, the purpose and limit of which it is
not for us puny mortals to define.   Creatures whose
flesh is most esteemed as food, are, physically, our
counterparts; the same high nervous organization,
the sensitiveness to physical suffering, terror, and
dread, with a still acuter sense of approaching death.

(To be continued.)

Society Reports.

THE VEGETARIAN SOCIETY, NEW YORK.

EXECUTIVE COMMITTEE FOR 1896.

President, JOHN WALTER SCOTT.
First Vice-President, MRS. M. A. HAVILAND.
Second Vice-President, GEORGE BRUNSWICK.
Treasurer, CHARLES A. MONTGOMERY.
Secretary, ARTHUR HAVILAND.

Regular Meetings held on the fourth Tuesday in the month at 98 Fifth avenue.

60TH REGULAR MEETING.

At the 60th meeting of the Vegetarian Society, New York, held April 27, 1897, at 98 Fifth avenue, President J. W. Scott in the chair, twelve members and twenty-five visitors present, after approval of minutes of last meeting, Dr. E. G. Day, M. D., was introduced as the lecturer, who read an interesting, instructive and learned paper on "Health, physical, mental and spiritual," after which many questions were asked and answered, and the meeting adjourned.

A. HAVILAND, *Secretary.*

The Secretary of the Vegetarian Society, New York, wishes information as to places within 100 miles of the city, where good VEGETARIAN BOARD can be had. All are requested to aid in this inquiry.

THE
VEGETARIAN·

SUBSCRIPTION:

Per Year, prepaid, to any part of the World, ... 25 cents.
10 Subscriptions, to different addresses . . . . . . $1.00.
Single copies, 2 cents; 50 cents per 100.

Published Monthly by
The Vegetarian Publishing Company, 40 John Street, New York City.

Entered at the New York Post Office as Second-class matter.

VOL. II.   JUNE 15, 1897.   NO. 12.

Health.

BY E. G. DAY, M. D.

*Read before the Vegetarian Society, New York,
April 27, 1897.*

Continued from page 174.

The horrors to which these humbler members of the Father's great household are subjected in the abattoirs are equalled only by the atrocities of the inquisition. There are many who, once emancipated from the idea of the "necessary evil," would discard meat from choice, and *more* who, did they know the true story of the shambles, would *renounce* everything which encouraged such practises. Again, the brutalizing and blighting effects of the slaughter-house rests upon and goes forth with its inmates, warping their sensibilities, destroying their sympa-

thy and thick veiling the divinity within them.
They become unfit for social and domestic duty, and,
above all, disqualified for perpetuating a healthy
race. Blood and brutality, mingled with profanity,
must influence the forthcoming personality. These
are serious thoughts which cannot be ignored by anyone in whom exists a desire, however small, for the
elevation of the race. To return to our food table :—
I am aware that a very simple diet of vegetables,
and preferably, *fruits* and *nuts* would not be adapted
to one who has just abandoned the ordinary animal
food diet. The change from one system to the other
must be by gradations, gradually many articles will
be eliminated until finally a few well selected foods
will suffice.

Before one can make any progress in this dietary
path a lesson must be learned and a dominant desire
be conquered. The lesson is that more should *eat*
to "live" and not "*live*" to eat. The desire to be
subjugated is that insatiable appetite for endless *variety in food*. These are the initial steps for one who
would be emancipated from the slavery of palatal
appetite.

I can almost hear a chorus of voices exclaiming :—
"the simple diet which you advocate may be very
good but we would tire of those same things every
day:" Now the idea which is embodied in those
words ("tired of those same things every day") is
the *key* which explains why there are great markets,
crowded with varieties of food—why persons who
can prepare this food in countless ways receive from
$16 per month to $10,000 a year—why the leading
attraction at a hotel is its table—why skilled cater-

ers amass fortunes—why a merciless warfare is
waged on every living creature which is deemed fit
to enter man's stomach—why it is that ten thousand
intelligent women in this city alone have said to-day
" I declare I don't know what to get for the family
to eat," "what a trouble it is,"—why appeals for
charity are so often met by the expression " I would
be glad to do something, but it takes every cent I
can get to live,"—why it is that in the meat shops,
the bake shops, and at the fishmongers may daily be
met well dressed and intelligent appearing women
with anxious, careworn faces, not the outcome of
profound and prolonged thought upon the great
problem of man, his origin, and his destiny, but
rather man, his *appetite*, and how to satisfy it.

It is this insatiable greed in man for variety in
food which has reduced to a *galling serfdom* three-
fourths of the housekeepers of to-day. The slavery
to which our wives, mothers and sisters are subjected
by this *manly?* appetite is appalling. The grand possibility of woman's mind for culture and refinement,
and its power to set in action forces which must
ameliorate, reform and elevate the race, *forbid* that
its capabilities should be paralyzed by the constant
burden of *domestic trivialities*. Is it right that the
individualized ray of the universal mind so beautifully mirrored in woman should be exclusively ab-
sorbed with thoughts pertaining to food, personal
adornment and house decoration? In this wide domain are there not many fields of labor wherein, with
strong mentality, loving hope, true charity and deep
sympathy she may work for the betterment of the
present race, and the uplifting of those yet to come?

The reason for this is twofold. 1st. The desire for *palatal* indulgence which may become a sensuous gratification as baneful in its effects as others which are more emphatically criticised, and 2nd. the inability to realize that the costly Delmonico dainty will nourish the physical body no more, if as well, as the measure of nuts costing but a few cents. Once the interior wall of the pharynx is passed, the princely entree and the plebian nut drop into a common receptacle where their true worth is recognized. Many of our domestic animals, *notably* the workers, thrive on the same food day by day. Why should man, with the same organs, require such a complex diet?

Let us next consider, symbolically, the "good draft," which means, as applied to the animal body, plenty of *oxygen*—upon the supply of this gas all the physiological processes depend. Close the draft in the furnace and the fire becomes extinct. Shut off the supply of *oxygen* and the animal dies. With a poor draft the fire burns but feebly; with a reduced supply of oxygen the great physical processes of the body are impeded, or suspended. Sub-normal functional activity in an organ results in atrophy and ultimate diseases, which, if not arrested, terminate in death. Hence the importance of a *full supply of oxygen*. We have seen that the various tissues receive their supply of this gas through the lungs. No argument should be needed for *encouraging*, and not *impeding*, the supply of the vital air. Our lungs should have full *play;* every restriction on their free movement avoided. Persons who sit or walk erect breathe easier and deeper than those who stoop.

Men, as a rule, breathe better than women, hence, the disease known as Anemia—insufficiently oxygenated blood—is more common among the latter than the former. The bad habit which women have of encasing themselves in a modification of the medieval armor—with this difference however, whereas the armor was defensive, the ordinary corset is highly aggressive—is a prime cause of numerous ills which afflict the fair sex.

I have never, professionally, seen a woman who (in her opinion) wore a tight corset, yet it is a fact that 75 per cent. of those who thus encase themselves cannot take a full *inspiration*. Even if the corset is fairly easy, a deep breath will seriously tax the quality of the fabric in which the woman is clothed, or the devices which hold it in place. A well known physician of Brooklyn has carefully investigated the subject of corset pressure. He says, "the least pressure from a corset is 26℔s., the greatest 88℔s., the average 35℔s. Few women are strong enough to lift 88℔s. A sack of flour weighs 25℔s., or ten pounds less than the pressure of our ordinary corset. How many women can carry a sack of flour? Yet, here we have constant pressure on the vital organs of a weight which cannot be borne in the arms." The diaphragm, a great muscular partition dividing the thoracic from the abdominal cavity, is the principal muscle of respiration. In the average woman this muscle is not utilized, being so restricted by pressure as to be inoperative. It has been said that women pant with their costal muscles, while men breathe with their diaphragm. This difference may be observed by any one who will make the in-

vestigation.   Corset pressure exerts other baneful
influences.   Charts might be exhibited illustrating
the displacement of vital organs resulting in a change
of form and functions.   Sometimes the liver is forced
into the thoracic cavity, causing compression of the
lungs—a condition which I have witnessed at an au-
topsy—or, the spleen and pancreas are made to in-
vade the domain of the stomach; or the delicate and
reproductive organs are crowded into the pelvic
basin, causing loss of function and great discomfort
by their pressure on the " (sacral) plexus " of nerves.
All such abnormities are attended by a train of evils
which it would require more than one evening to re-
hearse.   Actuated by the false idea that their personal attractiveness is enhanced, women too often
attire themselves in a manner which disqualifies them
for those duties which are dependant upon good
health, and are inseparable from the true woman,
wife and mother, and causes them to degenerate
from the *highest* and *noblest* in the evolutionary
series into a *perambulating nervous wreck*, constantly
and mercilessly scourged either by a *chronic headache*
or *backache*.

I would plead with my fair sisters to be emancipated from the tyranny of fashions conceived in the
brains of inconsiderate Parisian modistes, to raise
superior to the many false conventionalities in dress,
to clothe themselves as nature—which makes no
mistakes—dictates, to recognize the Divinity within
them, and provide for Him a healthier, and hence
nobler, and more beautiful dwelling.

The corset is frequently worn to reduce, or disguise corpulency.   This is a mistake.   The steady

pressure on one zone of the abdomen induces increase
of adipose tissue above and below that line, this increases rather than diminishes the evil. Permit me
to say incidentally, that the wearing of heavy apparel
supported by the hips is scarcely less injurious than
the corset. Every means should be employed—by
both sexes—to increase the capacity of the chest.
This may be accomplished by deep inhalation and
slow respiration, by the systematic use of light
"dumb-bells," and well balanced "indian clubs," by
calisthenics, and judicious gymnastics. Did time
permit, I might tell you something about the "*Science
of Breath*" on the physical plane; how increased
respiration raises the bodily temperature, and may
be employed to prevent a "cold" during exposure,
how it is a potent influence in dispersing an abnormal
pulmonary condition, how it may be used to allay
pain, calm nervous excitement, and remove *insomnia*,
etc., but we must pass to the symbolical "*smoke
flue*," which means physiologically, the elimination
of the *waste products* from the body through the
agencies already named. These substances, if retained, undergo decomposition, with the release of
poisonous matter, which, in time, may infect the
system through the blood and produce septicæmia,
or blood poisoning. See to it that all the avenues of
exit are free. Everyone recognizes that a clogged
waste pipe in a house is dangerous and demands
prompt attention. Let me assure you that a like
condition in the animal body should arouse more ap-
prehension. Let the intestinal tract be flushed daily
by drinking plenty of water. The majority of the
human family do not consume enough of this pre-

cious fluid, and in consequence suffer from a long
train of ills.   Free use of water with daily exercise
will, ordinarily, keep the kidneys in normal condition, but at the first symptom of diminished energy
seek medical advice, for—speaking metaphorically—
these are the gates through which trains of ash carts
are hourly passing out.   As much rejected material
passes off through the skin in the form of insensible
perspiration, it is important that this sheath of the
delicate mechanism be kept in perfect condition.
This may be done by means of the *simple morning
bath.*   I would be glad to enlarge upon this particular subject did time permit.   It is astonishing that
so many persons have a catlike aversion to water.
I have had patients among the middle and upper
classes who positively declined to bathe daily.   The
flimsiest excuses would be urged in opposition.   One
woman actually asserted that it made her sick.   This
kind of opposition to a sanitary measure is, ordinarily, the offspring of indolence and incorrect parental
education.   The daily morning bath with cool water
is stimulating, and is one of the surest prophylactics
against *colds in the head,* larynx and lungs, sore
throat, etc., and generally prevents those disagreeable chilly sensations which afflict so many.   Garments worn next the body during the day should be
removed and well aired at night.

The bad habit of sleeping in the underclothing has
its origin in a *fancied* increased comfort, or in that
indifference which seeks to abbreviate every duty.

The clothing, especially during sleep, becomes
saturated with cast off material.   To keep this in
contact with the body during the period of activity

is to invite reabsorption, a process similar to that which is possible in the intestinal tract and productive of like results. Those who find the ordinary night robe insufficient should substitute for it one made of light weight flannel. Remember, that as on a railroad, a block at one station may arrest all the trains on the line, so in the animal body, an abnormal condition of one organ may seriously impede the movement of those little "oxygen wagons," the red corpuscles of the blood which convey vitality to all parts of the system. Such interference always means disaster. Avoid it! Those ornamental, and useful, but abused members, the teeth, demand passing reference. It would be a quixotic person who applied at a mill for fine flour knowing that the mill stones were either cracked, broken, or absent. Quite as unreasonable is it to think that a properly conditioned bolus of food can be sent to the stomach from a mouth filled with broken and diseased teeth, or one from which the "grinders" have departed. There are certain animals which have gastric juice so strong that they can reduce large pieces of food without previous mastication, but the human family require finely comminuted food. Frequently a pronounced pathological condition may be traced to diseased teeth. I have been consulted by patients for relief from gastric or nervous ills, to whom my first instruction was to visit a dentist and have the sources of contamination removed.

It is a *lamentable fact* that some will neglect their teeth to adorn their bodies. Another great factor in the promotion of health, the importance of which cannot be overestimated, is *sleep*, "nature's sweet restorer." Surely if the soul requires rest in "the land of the hereafter," the worn and illused physical body needs periodical refreshing repose on earth. It is the period of relaxation from overstrain, during which the muscle and the nerve cell recruit their exhausted energy.

The minimum amount of sleep required by humanity is eight hours; the young and the aged require more. The practice of extending literary work, commercial activity, amusement and feverish excitement *far into the night* is abnormal and will abbreviate life. Far better would it be, imitating the example of our animal friends and our primitive brothers, to seek repose when the "sun god" sinks to rest, and be ready to meet and greet his advent on the ensuing morning.

After all I have treated this great subject of physical health in a very cursory manner. It would require more than one evening to take up the collateral branches exhaustively, for it is a subject with which able writers have filled many volumes.

In considering the subject of *mental health* we recognize a striking analogy between the laws which govern the body and those which apply to the *mind*. As physical health depends upon a normal body in which all the organs function harmoniously, and correlatively, so mental health implies a condition of well balanced intellectual faculties; a state in which all impressions received through the sense organs are properly translated, and never distorted. Distortion of sense perceptions constitutes hallucinations —one form of insanity. Persons in whom the mental faculties are not well *equilibrated* are usually recognized as "cranks," or, if this opprobrious title is not quite merited, the milder appellations of "peculiar" or "strange" seem to be fairly earned. This condition may result from an impoverished supply of blood food to that complex network of nerves, the *brain*. As it is through this organ that the mind must function on the physical plane, the clearness of the mental manifestations will be proportioned to the normal condition of this great nerve center. As the body requires the ingestion of suitable food, complete assimilation of its nutritive ingredients, and through elimination of its unappropriated materials, so the *mind* demands a nourishing, and developing mental pabulum, the appropriation of all which promotes growth, purifies and energizes, with the eradication of that which retards development and contaminates. Selection of mental aliment requires even more discrimination than in the choice of our physical diet. Carelessness and indifference in either case will be succeeded by undesirable consequences. In the domain of literature, including the "daily press" which not infrequently publishes—as news—highly sensational and unwholesome material, there is more to reject than to accept. There, as in the great family markets, we find articles wholy unfit for food, and which if ingested, must awaken forces of a very deleterious character. Impure writings breed corruption in the mind like tainted flesh within the body. Highly sensational literature, like the alcoholics, produces undue mental stimulation followed by impaired functional activity, and develops an abnormal appetite for more of the fascinating material. The "goody goody" weak literature, full

of platitudes and abounding in thoughts and advice
drawn from a very narrow Theology is equally objectionable, as it lacks mental nutriment and contributes to the mind about what the "tea and toast"
diet would supply to the body.

The question, What shall we read? arises naturally. I believe that our mental regimen should
comprise those articles which contain the maximum
amount of *truth* within the minimum amount of
error, from which the mind may receive nourishment
without exhaustion and stimulation, without subsequent depression. Let us seek it in the pages of
well authenticated history, judiciously arranged fiction, demonstrated science, synthetical theology and
logical metaphysics. As in current books, so in the
drama of the day. Research will reveal more that is
unwholesome than nutritious; more that produces
feverish fermentation than ennobling peace; more
that debases than exalts; more that poisons than
heals. In the realm of art we find more that is
sensuous than spiritual; more that excites the emotions than expands the heart; more that appeals to
the intellect than awakens response in the *soul*.
Even in the popular music of the day there is more
that fascinates than glorifies. Where shall we seek
an explanation? It is not to be found in the insatiable appetite of the human being for variety and
change; the restless discontent with what might
prove a merciful monotony; the inability to realize
that in the natural and the simple may be found that
which is eagerly sought in the abnormal, and the
complex.

Thought has a wondrous power to foster mental

health or engender mental disease. It is easier to
close the lips against deleterious articles of food than
to bar the avenues through which *thoughts* come and
go. Good thoughts, like the gentle rain, are purify-
ing, refreshing and upbuilding. Bad thoughts, like
pestilence, corrupt, demoralize and destroy. Like
miasma they breed disease and death. As well expect the charnal house to remain taintless with its
putrifying tenantry, as the mind to continue healthy
when surcharged with corrupt thoughts. And
thoughts are *entities*. Occultism has long known
that which science is beginning to realize. As they
go forth from us they are freighted with life or
death. They materialize. They become potencies
for good or evil. The corrupt mind cannot put forth
good thoughts any more than the corrupt tree can
bring forth good fruit. Shall we be thrifty plants
full of light and life "sending forth leaves for the
healing of the nations," or centers of infection ex-
haling disease and death. It is a question which we
cannot disregard.

When we approach the *Spiritual* aspect of health
we enter the domain of *something* which bears strong
likeness to that "vital air" so essential to the life
and welfare of the body, the soul, the vitalizing immortal spirit, the Divine ray which illuminates,
quickens, and directs the impermanent shifting personality during its earthly pilgrimage, the tremen-
dous *power* which separates man from the so-called
brute by a fathomless gulf which has never been
bridged, the *crown* which exhalts him so far above
the most intelligent of the lower order that the distance seems infinite, the mighty force which enables

him to wrest from nature her secrets and make them
subservient to his will, clutch the thunderbolt and
reduce it to servitude, from crude materials bring
forth the loom and cotton gin, the printing press,
steam engine, chronometer and telegraph, the *super-
human intelligence* which defines the orbits and
periods of the planets, calculates the parallax of stars
trillions of leagues away, charts the pathway of those
weird wonders through space, the *comets*, and unerr-
ingly designate their periodical visitations, tell the
story of the equinoxes, analyze the sunbeam, compose harmonies worthy of seraph choirs.

The mysterious something which impels man to
speculate on his origin, and destiny, the *radiance*
which illuminates the names of the great scientists
and spiritual teachers, the *divine attraction* which
draws man away from the comosine cares of earth
life, from the sorrow and disappointment which
sadden, from the ceaseless struggle with the varied
problems of life, from the delusive pleasures and excitement which beset the pilgrim's pathway, from
the unhealthy ambitions which, "ignis fatuus " like,
allure but to deceive, from all the *petty envy, jealousy,*
and *strife*, which corrupt the heart, and bid him *rest*.

Unless the mind is bathed in the divine radiance
of the spirit it can never manifest its glorious possi-
bilities, but must travel the narrow circle within
which the beast is circumscribed with those occasional flashes of spiritual life upon it which now and
then appear as remarkable intellectuality associated
with pronounced animalism, or, with a deeper glow
of the divine light resting upon, yet not permeating
i t, flash through its earth life with meteoric bril-

liancy, but leaving no trace of its course, no monument sacred to its memory, or, it may wander in darkness amidst the rocks and pitfalls of materialism vainly striving to ascribe the manifestations of the *nominal* in the phenomenal to the fortuitous grouping of blind forces, rather than to the immutable operations of Divine law. From *spirit* all proceeds, and into spirit all eventually returns. In the long ascending path through the kingdom of nature everything was born of spirit. In endless cycles spirit descends with matter and reascends to the Divine, as beautifully symbolized in Jacob's dream. In the spirit is the *initial* point where true and perfect health has its origin. Bestow upon the body all possible care, employ every means for physical development, disregarding the mind and the spirit, and perfect health will not be secured. To the carefully nurtured body add high intellectual culture, still, ignoring the influence of the spirit and yet true health will not be attained. Only when we have risen to and become suffused with the spiritual light of our " Higher Selves "—the Divine ray from the Father—will we possess the requisite *knowledge*, *desire* and *will power* to put in action those controlling, and determining forces which create and regulate perfect health. Prominent among these is the ability to concentrate the mind upon a single point, to exclude all sense perceptions, to meditate so deeply that a realization of the oneness of the individual with the Divine is established, and then by forming strong and vivid pictures of a perfect manhood, release agencies which will produce conditions wherein essays on physical health will not be required. Then and not until then will cease that restless, detrimental desire for variety and change; then will fade that insatiable yearning for the pleasures of the senses; then will the discord, born of unattained ambitions, be succeeded by the holy harmony of contentment; then will our strong grasp upon the things of time, and sense relax as we clasp the things which are eternal; then will we see with spiritual vision the *unsatisfactory* lives we have led, and realize the darkness from which we have emerged.

Then will the restless discontent of our personality be transformed into an *enduring peace*.

www.ingramcontent.com/pod-product-compliance
Lightning Source LLC
Chambersburg PA
CBHW030551040726
47497CB00008B/2670